WOTTA REV

The rat jumped ou

the floor.

Ben Grimm made a face.

Living in New York, you saw just about everything, but this . . .

A rat hitching a ride in somebody's coat pocket? That was a new one, even on him.

The rat flopped around a minute; one of its legs was all twisted up funny. There was something else wrong with it, too; it kept shaking, like it was having convulsions. There was blood matted in with its fur, some other stuff, too. Looked like rat guts. *Blecch.*

"Wotta revolting development," Ben said under his breath.

Though it wasn't the rat's fault, the way it looked. Musta gotten hit by a car or something. Poor little thing was beat to hell. Bleeding, and that leg . . . it was dying, obviously.

Ben raised a foot to put it out of its misery.

The rat looked up at him.

"Don't," it said.

Ben froze with his foot in midair.

He blinked.

Talking rats. That was a new one on him, too.

FANTASTIC FOUR®

The Baxter Effect

a novel by
Dave Stern

based on the
Marvel Comic Book

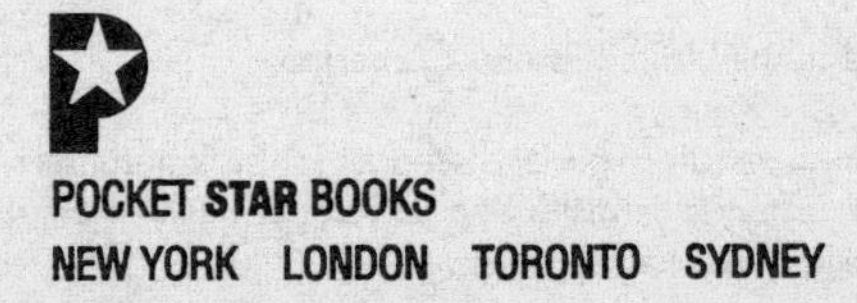

An *Original* Publication of POCKET BOOKS

A Pocket Star Book published by
POCKET BOOKS, a division of Simon & Schuster, Inc.
1230 Avenue of the Americas, New York, NY 10020

ISBN-13: 978-1-4165-1066-6
ISBN-10: 1-4165-1066-4

This Pocket Star Books paperback edition January 2007

10 9 8 7 6 5 4 3 2 1

Design by John Vairo Jr.; Art by Glen Orbik

Manufactured in the United States of America

"If you want to survive . . . you must be a devil."

—*Old Gypsy proverb*

Prologue

Clack-clack, clack-clack, clack-clack.

Machine-gun fire. Shouts of pain, of anger and surprise, followed by the screams of grown women, the sobs of old men.

Nine-year-old Olga Javelka ran for her life.

She heard a whistling sound over her head, growing louder and louder, and then there was a huge explosion, a wave of heat and dust and pulverized stone catching her from behind, nearly lifting her off her feet, the sound and feel of the refugee camp she called home being destroyed by the KLA, the Albanian soldiers chasing them from this side of Kosovo just as a half dozen years earlier the Serbs had chased them from the other, for no reason at all. No reason other than their own superstitious fears and the blood that ran in the veins of Olga's people, the blood that the Albanians and Serbs, like the Hapsburgs and the Nazis and the Spaniards and all the peoples of Europe before them, were all too eager to shed. Outsiders' blood. Strangers' blood.

Gypsy blood.

"We are Roma," Grandma Irina had said on that day when she adopted Olga for her own, after the Serbs had killed the little girl's parents. "That is why."

And then Grandma, who believed in the old Roma ways as Olga's parents never had, placed an amulet around the little girl's neck, a necklace of colored beads and coral, with a disk of dull copper metal at the end of it.

The amulet had a name, she told Olga. The amulet was called *K'ol Byola.*

The amulet was magic.

It was gypsy magic, the magic of their ancestors. Magic meant to be used as protection, *bahtali,* white magic, which was all Grandma Irina performed. Never would she use *bibahtali,* the black magic of the Gypsy King in the East, whose name she dared not speak, whose actions since taking power had caused people the world over to fear the Roma more than ever.

The amulet was to safeguard her against just such magics, from evil in all its aspects, evil spirits that might arise to plague her.

"Me?" Olga asked. "Why would evil spirits want to harm me?"

Because you are so good, Grandma Irina had said then, with a smile on her face. Because you are special. Besides, Irina went on, the amulet was to protect her from men as well, men and the machines they built.

If ever you are in danger, call upon the amulet. Call upon the power of *K'ol Byola*—the power of the circle. The power of life itself.

Clack-clack, clack-clack, clack-clack.

The machine guns sounded again, and no one was safe. The bullets found Grandma Irina, and she died, the amulet no match for the soldiers' weapons. Olga felt the magic rise in her and struck out without thinking, and now it was the Albanians screaming, the Albanians whose blood stained the ground of the refugee camp red.

Clack-clack, clack-clack, clack-clack.

The machine-gun fire slowed. The screams faded.

Olga Javelka—now twenty-three, a dozen years removed from the horrors of Kosovo—blinked and opened her eyes.

The subway car crawled to a stop. *Clack-clack, clack-clack, clack-clack,* and the doors of the F train opened onto the empty platform at Fourth Avenue. No passengers—not a surprise this early in the morning, the sky graying only slightly in anticipation of full sunrise. All she saw was cracked cement, rusted steel beams—industrial decay. Kosovo all over again.

Under the fluorescent platform lights, a rat scurried past on the platform. Olga started.

A second followed the first, and then a third, all coming so close to the car that for an instant, Olga feared they would run inside. She shuddered at the thought . . . she had been that close to vermin before, in Kosovo, she knew what they could do, what they would do, if . . .

The doors closed, and the train started again.

Clack-clack, clack-clack, clack-clack.

Olga looked up and saw she was alone in the car. Two women had been riding with her when she'd gotten on; they must have gotten off sometime while she'd been dozing. Not a problem, though. She was in the conductor's car, where she always rode on these early mornings when she had to be first at Theo's. Just a step away from the conductor's door. Any problems, all she had to do was bang on his door.

The F slowed and stopped again. Smith and Ninth Streets. Another chill wind, another empty platform, another rat dashed by the door. They were unusually bold this morning—driven by the cold, she decided. It almost seemed, somehow, as if they were trying to get up the courage to enter the subway car.

Ridiculous.

The doors closed, and the train picked up speed again, heading downhill from Park Slope toward the East River, the last little bit of track that ran aboveground before they entered the tunnels for the trip into Manhattan. Olga turned in her seat to catch a glimpse of the city skyline, that fairy-tale landscape, the one she'd dreamed of when she was a little girl, the place she'd somehow known she would end up, her destiny, though now that she worked there, fourteen hours a day, six days a week, fifty-one weeks a year . . .

There wasn't quite so much fairy tale to it. Especially on an early morning like this, especially after sleepless nights like the one she'd just had. The dreams, the same ones that had continued this morning, Grandma Irina, the Albanians, the *bibahtali* inside her, the shooting, the screaming . . . scenes from her past mixed in with scenes from her present, images of the people she waited on at Theo's, the fancy ladies, their fancy men, the Super Heroes she sometimes saw, capable of magic just like her grandmother, except they called their magic science.

Olga turned away from the window and barely—just barely—stifled a scream.

There was a man sitting across from her.

A black man, in a multicolored robe, barefoot. Twenty degrees, and he was barefoot. And where had he come from? When had he . . .

Rats.

Dozens of rats—too many to count—on the seat to either side of him, crawling on him, gathered at his feet . . .

He looked at her, confusion in his eyes.

"This is wrong," he said. "I should be right at the

building, I should be . . ." He shook his head back and forth. "This is wrong."

One of the rats scampered up his arm, perched on his shoulder. He paid it no mind, just kept shaking his head.

The look in his eyes . . . he was crazy, clearly. A crazy man snuck onto the train when she wasn't looking, no reason to be scared, he was harmless, except . . .

For some reason, she was terrified.

The man's gaze found hers, and she felt a strange tickling in the back of her head—inside her head.

"Javelka," the man said. "Olga Javelka."

My mind, she thought. *He just read my mind.*

She screamed.

He raised a hand and pointed it at her, and she felt invisible fingers tighten around her throat, and that scream died in her mouth.

"Don't be scared, Olga," the man said, the confusion suddenly gone from his gaze. He rose to his feet and stood over her. "I mean you no harm."

The grip on her neck relaxed and suddenly let go. She gasped for air.

The man stared at her intently.

"Maybe not so wrong after all," he said.

She had no idea what he meant.

"Many strands, Olga. All leading here—to you. Probabilities, some might say." He spoke slowly, as if he were trying to explain something to her.

The rats skittered down from the seat and pooled

around his feet, like a thousand and one trained dogs.

His feet. They weren't touching the ground. He was floating in air.

Bibahtali, she thought, and in her mind, she pictured the sorcerer who now ruled her country.

Olga shrank back in her seat.

"Please," she said. "Please leave me alone."

He shook his head.

"I am no Doom, Olga. You have nothing to fear from me."

He waved his hand, and the rats scattered.

"My name is Jembay Diehl, and my appearance here is accidental; I was intending to . . ."

The train jerked to a sudden, violent halt.

Olga reached out to try to brace herself, and failed. Her head slammed into one of the steel support poles. Her ears rang. Her vision swam.

She looked up and saw the man standing motionless above her, in exactly the same spot he'd been a second earlier, though now he was turned to face the front of the car. Perhaps she was imagining it, but Olga thought his face a shade paler than it had been a moment earlier.

"You're not imagining it," he said, and set his jaw. "Run, Olga." He nodded his head toward the back of the train. "Run as fast, as far as you can."

Coming from the front of the train, she heard the sound of glass being smashed and faintly muffled screams. The car trembled.

"I don't understand," she said. "What's happening?"

"He's here." The man slid backward without moving his feet. He raised his arms, as if to defend himself. "He's found me."

Olga turned to the front of the train.

The smashing sounds got louder. So did the screams.

"Run!" the man said again.

Olga ran.

She was halfway to the back of the car when the door behind her exploded, shards of metal and glass flying through the air, hitting the car walls and windows with a sound like falling hail. Olga couldn't help herself—she turned around.

Just in time to see a monster step into the car.

It had the shape of a man, but it wasn't a man at all, it was a thing of some kind, with gray skin, thick, misshapen, strange-looking limbs, and its face . . .

It had no face, just a smooth gray surface where its eyes and nose and mouth should have been.

The thing spoke.

"Jembay Diehl," it said, and began advancing on him.

"Thinker," he said. "I don't know how you found me—"

"Probabilities, Jembay." The thing walked as if it were made of stone; the car floor shook with each step it took. "There was a ninety-two-point-eight-percent chance you would decide to contact Richards today, a ninety-eight-percent chance you would do so well in advance of the experiment, and so I simply . . ."

Diehl motioned with his hands, and the rats attacked.

They exploded from everywhere—from seats behind and in front of the creature, from the floor around it, making all manner of impossible leaps to get at their intended target. It was like watching a swarm of ants on a dead animal. In the blink of an eye, every square inch of the creature was covered.

The thing paid them no mind whatsoever.

It stepped on the ones in its path as it walked; they made horrible squashing, squeaking noises as they died.

It slammed its arms into the seat backs and poles, and the rats fell from it like drops of rain, leaving slick crimson smears on the steel.

"You should have heeded my warnings, Jembay," the thing said. "You should have stayed away."

"What you intend is monstrous," Diehl said, and now, Olga saw, he was not just floating around the car, he was flying, flitting about like a bird trying to escape. "It must be stopped."

"And who, I wonder, will do that? You?" The creature's voice held a note of scorn.

"If I have to," Diehl said, and raised his right hand.

A beam of blue fire shot out from it. The fire struck the creature in the shoulder, and there was a sudden explosion and a burst of light and smoke.

When the smoke cleared, where the thing had been hit, Olga saw wires and a tangle of melted circuits.

It wasn't a monster.

It was a machine.

The creature turned its head toward the damaged area on its shoulder, as if to study it.

"Futile," it said, and the wires began moving of their own accord, knitting themselves together. A second later, the damaged area was whole again.

The creature turned to Jembay and resumed its advance.

Olga turned and ran toward the door at the end of the car. She grabbed the handle and pulled.

Locked.

She looked through the glass; a handful of people in the next car back were pressed up against the door, trying to see what was happening.

"Help!" she screamed, and banged on the door.

They looked at her strangely.

She heard a sudden, sickening thump behind her and turned to see the creature standing over a fallen Diehl, who was gripping his side and gasping in pain, holding one arm up before him as if to fend off the monster.

It drew back an arm to hit him again.

"No!" Olga screamed at the top of her lungs.

The creature's head snapped around, turning toward her.

"Query," it said. "Who are you?"

Diehl used the instant of distraction to gather his strength; again, blue fire flashed, much brighter this time. Olga saw the creature stagger for an insant; her vision blurred.

When it cleared, the monster stood perhaps half a foot farther back from Diehl, otherwise unharmed.

"Goodbye, Jembay Diehl," it said, and reached down with one hand and dragged the man to his feet.

Diehl had a strange, curiously blank expression on his face—as if he weren't there at all. He looked depleted; completely, utterly exhausted. Defeated.

At his feet, a single rat looked up and squeaked plaintively.

The monster reared back and struck Diehl with a single blow. Olga heard a sickening crack.

Diehl flew backward through the air, slammed into the wall of the subway car, and slid to the floor.

The creature leaned over him, held out a hand.

"Analysis. Respiratory function, negative. Circulatory function, negative. Brain function, negative. Time of death: five-twelve A.M."

A noise halfway between a gasp and a whimper escaped Olga's throat. The monster turned to her.

"Who are you?" the creature repeated, and took a step in her direction.

She felt the metal door against her back; she slid slowly to the floor.

"Don't," she said.

The monster towered over her.

"There is a point-three-seven-percent possibility your presence here is nontrivial," it said. "Recommended course of action: elimination."

"Oh, God," she said, and closed her eyes.

Gunfire.

The thing turned.

Behind it, Olga saw a handful of transit policemen, arms raised.

"Whatever the frack you are," the nearest of those cops said, his voice trembling, "don't move."

"Possibility of capture, point four one percent. Possibility of further identification, point six two percent," the monster said, and then seized Diehl's corpse, jumped up through the roof of the subway car, and disappeared.

The policemen rushed to her side.

"Miss?" she heard. "Miss, are you all right?"

She looked up at them, managed a weak smile, and fainted.

1

Ben Grimm flipped past the spread on page six, headlined "Web-Slinger Now a Web Menace," and turned to page fourteen, as the cover of the *Bugle* had told him to. And there it was, in black-and-white: "Yancy Street Demolition Scheduled."

He read the article. It was true, he saw; a whole block of Yancy Street brownstones, the block between McGraw and Stanton, was coming down, a new multiplex was going up. He shook his head. Those old buildings were falling apart, it was true, more of the windows had boards over them than glass, the only people who lived there now were the old ladies and the gang members, but still . . .

That old block was home. That was where he'd grown up after his parents died, where he and his older brother, Dan, God rest his soul, had played football in the street, hung out late nights on the stoop, watched out for the little kids coming home from school . . .

It wasn't right. Turning a whole neighborhood into a shopping mall. But what could you do? It was happening all over the city. Manhattan was a place for rich people now, you couldn't live here unless you hit the six-figure mark, and who made that kind of money?

Well . . . he did, but that was hardly the point. Not a lot of people would want his job—well, they might want it, but they wouldn't want to go through what he had to get it.

Ben read on and saw with some satisfaction that the company doing the demolition work was having trouble staying on schedule; somebody kept stuffing potatoes in their bulldozer's tailpipe. "A dangerous, dangerous, stunt," according to Vito Lungati of the Pasqualone Construction Company. "Not funny at all. Somebody could lose an eye. These pranksters oughtta keep that in mind."

Good old Yancy Street, Ben thought, and took a sip of his coffee.

Cold.

He looked up.

"Theo!"

The man at the counter—burly, unshaven, wearing a white shirt with "Manager" monogrammed above the pocket—turned and frowned.

"What you want?"

Ben raised his cup.

The man frowned.

"Coffee?"

"Yeah, coffee," Ben said.

Theo took his cup and filled it, looking angry the whole time. Ben shook his head and looked down at his plate. He'd ordered steak and eggs, half a dozen of them, over easy, rye toast, and orange juice.

He got grapefruit, whole wheat, and the eggs. After asking three times, Ben gave up on the steak.

Breakfast wasn't usually like this; they knew what he liked here, had the steak on the grill for him before he was sitting down, the juice and coffee right at his spot at the end of the counter. Theo made a good steak, too. But today Theo's kid was on the grill, a tall, weedy teenager with long hair, strands of which Ben had pulled out of his eggs, and Theo was at the counter, serving customers.

And Olga, his usual waitress, was nowhere to be seen. It was like some kind of omen.

Ben sighed and took a sip of his coffee, and almost spat it out.

"What the—"

Theo looked at him and frowned.

"What is matter?"

"Matter? Did you taste this?"

Theo's face reddened. "Is good coffee."

"It's dishwater." Ben held up his cup. "Weakest cup of joe I ever had in my life."

Theo glared.

His son leaned through the little opening from the kitchen.

"Yo, Dad, I told you to use two of those packs. That's what Olga does." The boy turned to Ben. "I told him, you know?"

Outta the mouths of babes, Ben thought, and managed a half-smile.

Theo glared at both of them—and then he looked over Ben's shoulder, toward the entrance to the coffee shop, and his face got even redder.

Ben followed his gaze and saw Olga hurrying through the door.

Theo started yelling.

"What you do, huh?" He put his hands on his hips. "You know what time it is? You see what time it is? You see what's happening?" He gestured toward the tables. "Place is madhouse, and where are you, hey? Where are you? Late is where. Late!"

"I'm sorry," Olga said, coming toward them, taking off her coat as she went. "I'm so sorry. There was an accident—there was this monster on the train, the police they asked me questions, they took me to the hospital, I kept saying I had to come to work, but—"

"Hospital?" Ben stood up, blocking her path to the

counter. He looked down. Olga had a bruise on her temple. She looked pale and a little woozy. "What happened? What's this about a monster?"

"It's nothing," she said. "Really. I'm fine now."

Ben shook his head. He'd been coming to Theo's weekday mornings for about three months now, and Olga had waited on him every one of those mornings. They weren't exactly friends, but he knew her well enough to take a little interest in her affairs. Especially if she wouldn't.

"You don't look so hot to me. I think you oughtta go back home, take it easy."

"She got to work." Theo peered around Ben and shook a finger at Olga. "She got to work. Place is madhouse, you see what's happening? Madhouse!"

"Hey." Ben raised his voice. He turned around.

He stood over Theo, all six-foot-one, five hundred fifty orange-rock pounds of himself, and now it was his turn to shake a finger.

"I think you oughtta take it easy, too, Theo."

The man gulped and took a step back.

Olga put a hand on Ben's arm.

"No, Mister Grimm. Really. I'm okay."

He turned, and looked her over again. Okay. She was pale, no doubt about it, and she did have that bruise, but otherwise . . .

"I can work," she said. "I need to work. I need this job."

She looked pretty certain about that.

"Okay," Ben said. "But when you got a minute, I wanna hear about what happened."

"Yes." She nodded. "When I have a minute."

She moved past him, headed behind the counter.

"Coat," Theo said, nodding at hers. "Hang it up, please."

He gestured toward the row of hooks on the wall.

"Here," Ben said. "Lemme take it for you."

She flashed him a grateful smile. "Thank you, Mister Grimm."

"Ben," he said.

She nodded. "Okay. Ben."

He took her coat.

A rat jumped out of its pocket and landed on the floor.

Olga screamed.

Theo shouted and took a step back.

Ben made a face.

Living in New York, you saw just about everything, but this . . .

A rat hitching a ride in somebody's coat pocket? That was a new one, even on him.

The rat flopped around a minute; one of its legs was all twisted up funny. There was something else wrong with it, too; it kept shaking, like it was having convulsions. There was blood matted in with its fur, some other stuff, too. Looked like rat guts. *Blecch.*

"Wotta revolting development," Ben said under his breath.

Though it wasn't the rat's fault, the way it looked.

Musta gotten hit by a car or something. Poor little thing was beat to hell. Bleeding, and that leg . . . it was dying, obviously.

Ben raised a foot to put it out of its misery.

The rat looked up at him.

"Don't," it said.

Ben froze with his foot in midair.

He blinked.

Talking rats. That was a new one on him, too.

"Say what?"

The rat gasped and took a breath. "Give me a minute," it said.

He looked at it. He looked over at Olga, whose eyes were still wide, and at Theo, who had come out from behind the counter with a big kitchen knife and was heading straight for the rat, and he held up his hand.

Theo stopped in his tracks.

"Put down the knife," Ben told him.

"It's a rat."

"It's a talking rat."

Theo glared. Ben looked back down to the floor.

"Okay," he said. "What do you need a minute for?"

"This," the rat said, and all at once, there was a flash of light and the smell of something burning.

Ben blinked, and instead of the rat, a man lay on the floor. Black guy. Big guy, as far as regular people went, maybe six and a half feet tall, wearing colored robes, with some sort of beads around his neck. Some kind of magician, obviously.

Ben knelt down next to him. He looked, all at once, familiar.

"I've come a long way to see you, Mister Grimm."

"Why?"

"I . . ." The man gasped again and shut his eyes for a second.

The same leg was twisted up beneath him that had been twisted on the rat. Twisted up, most likely broken, and that wasn't all that was wrong with the guy. There was a light sheen of sweat all over him; he looked as if he was in a lot of pain.

He looked as if—though Ben was no doctor—he was dying.

"Easy, buddy," Ben said, and put a hand on his arm. "We're gonna get you a doctor, and . . ."

"No time for that. No time at all. I—" he began, and then was seized by a sudden fit of coughing that came from so deep inside him Ben thought he was going to bring up a lung.

And then he did bring up blood, a thin trickle of it that escaped from the side of his mouth as the cough subsided.

Ben looked up. A woman in a business suit was talking on a cell phone, hand cupped over her mouth.

"Hang up and call an ambulance," he said. "Now."

The woman blanched, and her mouth froze open in midsentence.

"Ahhh . . ." she managed.

"Now," Ben said again.

She nodded and started punching keys on her phone.

"That's him," a voice said from behind him.

Ben turned and saw Olga staring at the man on the floor.

"Him. Who him? Whattaya mean?"

She shook her head. "Him. The man from the train, from before. When the monster attacked."

"This guy is the monster?" Ben asked.

Olga shook her head again. "No, no. He was with the rats. The monster attacked him."

Ben was confused.

"Sort this out for me, will ya?" he said to Olga. "This guy . . ."

A hand grabbed at his arm.

"You have to tell Richards," the man said. "You have to tell him to stop the experiment."

Ben frowned.

"I don't know what you're talking about," he said.

"The strands will come apart—you have to tell him not to do it." The man tried to sit up. Ben eased him back down.

"The strands," Ben agreed. "I will definitely tell him. You bet."

In the distance, he heard sirens. The ambulance on its way.

"Now, you sit back down," Ben told the man. "Just take it easy."

The man nodded.

"Easy," he said, and closed his eyes, and died.

2

FLYNN PULLED THE SHEET OVER THE DEAD GUY'S head and nodded to the EMTs, who lifted the stretcher and headed off with the body.

"Jembay Diehl." Flynn—Sergeant Richie Flynn, who was one of the top enforcement guys over at Building Twelve on Rikers Island, where they put the supervillain types who weren't powerful enough to warrant a trip out to the Vault in Colorado—stood up and turned to Ben. "A.k.a. Hoodoo Guru, a.k.a. Black Hand, a.k.a. a pain in my ass. Guy got out three weeks ago, never checked in with his parole officer, we've had an APB out on him for the last ten days."

"He was some kind of magician, right?"

"Yeah." Flynn looked down at the little gizmo in his hand and read off it. "Strictly small-time—a couple museum robberies in the eighties, tried to steal some artifacts out of one of those Upper East Side embassies . . . stuff like that. Dazzler caught him in"—he squinted at the screen—"March '88. Guy's been locked up since."

"Museums?" Ben frowned and peered over Flynn's shoulder. "You sure we're talking about the same guy? 'Cause the one I was talking to, he didn't seem like the 'worldly possessions' type."

"They're all worldly possessions types when you get down to it. But here—have a look for yourself."

Flynn held out the little gadget. There was a picture on the screen. "Rikers ID 12 Orange 879," *12* referring to the building, *Orange* to the ward, *879* to the inmate whose picture was on the screen, a younger version of the man Ben had just watched die, no doubt about it.

"I guess prison changed him," Ben said.

"Hard time will do that to a man." Flynn put the gadget away. "So what's this experiment he wants Reed to stop?"

Ben frowned. "Beats me. The only thing I know about . . . some government people are coming up to the lab for a demonstration later, a new computer Reed's been working on. Not really an experiment, though."

"That's gotta be it," Flynn said.

"I guess." Ben shrugged. "Unless he was just crazy. The way he was talking . . ."

"Strands." Flynn nodded. "You said. Still. Somebody was trying to stop him from trying to get to you."

"Some thing, you mean," Ben said.

"Maybe. Girl said some kind of robot . . . we only got her word on that part of it, though."

"You got the train car. That's pretty messed up, right?"

"Right. So maybe a robot. Maybe another nut job with a hyperactive metabolism. Who knows? Still . . . you ought to talk to Reed. Just in case."

"Oh, I will," Ben said. "You can count on that."

They talked a minute longer. Ben checked in on Olga, who was herself being checked over by another EMT, and then he pulled Theo aside and made sure he understood that when the EMTs were finished with his waitress, she was going straight home for a day off, no ifs, ands, buts, or second shifts about it. Theo nodded grumpily.

"Send me over Diehl's file when you get back to the office, okay?" Ben asked Flynn.

"Why wait?" The man shrugged. "I'll send it to you now."

Flynn punched a few buttons on his little gizmo and then told Ben the file was waiting for him on the FF's private server, available to access at his convenience.

Ben thanked him, said his goodbyes, and left the coffee shop.

He tried to remember a little more about the

demonstration Reed had going on this morning. A fancy new computer—he couldn't figure out how turning on a computer posed any sort of threat, though, to be honest, the details about Reed's new gadget were a little fuzzy in his head. He'd been preoccupied yesterday when Stretch was telling him about it. Alicia had said she was going to call, because they were thinking about going to a chamber music concert last night, and as much as Ben found listening to chamber music a little bit like watching paint dry, if Alicia was there—

He pushed open the lobby door to the Baxter Building and frowned.

Something was happening.

The lobby was crammed full of people—wall-to-wall business suits everywhere he looked, and none of them happy.

Over at the security desk, O'Hoolihan was arguing with one of them. Ben started in their direction.

"—exactly what you said ten minutes ago." The man—a little guy, five-seven tops—jabbed his finger at O'Hoolihan's chest. "So why don't you get back on the phone and find out what is going on?"

The little guy glared.

O'Hoolihan, who had a good six inches and sixty pounds on him, smiled. Ben knew that smile. It was O'Hoolihan's way of saying, "Good thing I'm working, otherwise I'd have to knock your head off and get my nice new coat dirty."

"I spoke to an engineer not two minutes ago, sir,"

O'Hoolihan was saying. "He assured me they're working as fast as they can."

The man glared. "Well, get on the phone and tell them to go faster."

"I don't think that would do much good, sir," O'Hoolihan said. "Why don't we give them a few more minutes, and then . . ."

The man slapped his hand down on the security desk. "I got a better idea. Why don't you do your job and get these goddamn elevators running again!"

O'Hoolihan's smile wavered just a fraction of an inch.

"My job, is it?" he said quietly. "My job, you say?"

Uh-oh, Ben thought.

The Baxter Building was home to a number of the city's most high-powered people—real estate brokers, lawyers, investment bankers, security analysts—type-A types, every one of them, a lot of them jerks, but they paid a premium for sharing office space with the Fantastic Four, and that money went into the group's bank account, so . . .

Ben considered it his job to defuse situations like these.

"We got a problem here?"

O'Hoolihan looked up.

"Mr. Grimm."

The little guy turned around and did a double-take. "Holy . . . the Thing. Wow. The Thing."

The Thing. Ben hated it when people called him

that. He kept picturing that hand from the Addams Family.

"Yeah. Thing. That's me. We got a problem here?"

He looked over at O'Hoolihan, who shook his head. "No problem, Mister Grimm. I'm just explaining to Mister Bruggles here—"

"Wow." The little guy—Bruggles—kept staring at Ben. "The guys will never believe this. I mean, I know you're in the building, but . . . you know, I didn't ever think I'd see you. Any of you guys. The Fantastic Four. And here you are, right?"

Ben nodded. "Here I am, right."

"Right." The guy kept smiling. "Hey. You know what? You think I could get your autograph? For my kid, I mean? He would flip out."

Bruggles rustled in his pocket for a pen. Ben looked him over. The man wore an eight-hundred-dollar suit, two-hundred-dollar shoes, and no wedding ring.

He doesn't have a kid, Ben decided. He was gonna get the autograph and hawk it on eBay.

"Can't do it, friend," Ben said, shaking his head and putting on what he hoped was an apologetic smile. "Noncompete clause, you know what I'm saying? With the owners of the gift shop." He nodded across the lobby, to the last store on the arcade, the FF's official gift shop. He actually had no idea whether they sold anything autographed, but they'd paid a nice chunk of change for the rights to sell official FF merchandise, so . . .

Bruggles looked disappointed. Ben looked to O'Hoolihan. "So what's going on? What are all these people doing here?"

"Ah." O'Hoolihan shook his head in disgust. "Some kinda problem with the passenger elevators. Can't get 'em to come up from the parking garage under the building. They got 'em all shut down now, tryin' to figure it out."

"Which I'm sure they'll do in a minute. Hang in there, Mister Bruggles. We'll have you back at work in a jiffy." Ben clapped the man on the shoulder—lightly—and Bruggles stumbled forward, trying to stay upright. *There,* Ben thought. *There's a story for your kid, or your buddies at work, whatever. The Thing patted you on the back.*

He nodded to O'Hoolihan, gave him a thumbs-up and a "hang in there" as well, and turned toward the FF's private elevator, which ran off an entirely separate circuit from the passenger cars in the rest of the building. The doors opened automatically at his approach—thanks to a chip in his belt buckle—and Ben entered the car without breaking stride.

Six point six seconds later, forty floors higher, he walked onto C level, where the lab was, and stopped in his tracks.

He was too late. The demonstration had already started.

Reed stood at the far end of the lab, on a stage a few feet high, before a crowd of about two dozen people, half of them in uniform—army, air force. Behind him was a curtain, drawn shut. Next to him was a machine of some kind, maybe seven feet tall, that big around again. The side of it facing the audience was a clear panel; through the panel, Ben saw a large display screen, with a full-size picture of . . .

Himself.

Ben frowned.

"—so while ordinary computers work with binary information, bits of data that are either on or off, this machine," Reed said as he tapped the side of the box before him, "uses Q-bits, which can exist in several different states at once."

"Which I still don't see how is possible." One of the military types up front—an older man, white-haired, chewing on a cigar, which of course wasn't lit. Reed had this thing about no cigars in the lab, which Ben had tried a couple of times to talk him out of, particularly after they got those Cubans from Valdez after the Guantánamo thing, but Reed wasn't budging. "How can something exist in several different states at once?"

"It's like your budget, General," someone else in the audience said.

Everyone laughed—except for the general. Ben recognized him—Ross. Thunderbolt Ross, they called him: he had some kind of connection to the Hulk, Ben had never entirely puzzled out.

"It does seem counterintuitive, doesn't it?" Reed said. "But it's precisely because of the Q-bit's unique properties that I've been able to construct this prototype."

"Which is going to give me my unbreakable cipher," the general said.

"Among other things," Reed said. "This computer will enable us to map out the human genome in seconds, predict the weather down to half a degree. The processors in here are literally millions of times more powerful than anything else on the planet."

"Huh." The older man didn't look convinced.

"It's all right if you don't entirely believe it, General. Einstein himself didn't like the idea. 'God doesn't play dice with the universe,' he said—but in fact, quantum mechanics tells us that's what goes on, every day."

Ben was about to speak up when he saw Sue, standing with Jasper Sitwell off to his left, to the side of the crowd. He walked over to join them.

"Ben, you remember Jasper," Sue said as he approached.

"Sure." Sitwell was from S.H.I.E.L.D., one of Nick Fury's boys. Well, he'd been a boy when Ben first met him, barely out of college, big thick glasses, looked a little like Truman Capote's little brother. Now he'd filled out. Bulked up.

"How you doin', Sitwell?" he asked.

"Excellent. Filled with anticipation. Anxious to see the computer at work."

Sue smiled. "As we all are. It won't be too much

longer." She looked at Ben, and the smile turned to a frown. "Something the matter?"

"Not sure," Ben said, and filled her in—the monster on the subway, the talking rat in the coffee shop, Diehl's cryptic warning.

"So you need to talk to Reed," she said when he'd finished.

He nodded. She turned, raised her head maybe half an inch, her eyebrows even less, and just like that, Reed, in the middle of talking more about potential real-world uses for a quantum computer, stopped in midsentence and smiled apologetically.

"Excuse me a moment, ladies and gentlemen," he said, and walked off the stage, headed in Sue's direction.

Married people, Ben thought. *They got some kind of telepathy or something.*

"Sue. What is it?" Reed asked.

She stepped aside and let Ben explain.

"'Stop the experiment.'" Reed frowned. "I wouldn't call this an experiment, exactly. It's simply a public demonstration of something I've already used in private, on several different occasions."

"Right," Ben said. "But still—"

"In the second place," Reed continued, "Jembay Diehl. Hoodoo Guru. Black Hand. Very minor sorcerer. To the best of my recollection, he has no particular expertise in quantum physics."

"Well . . . no," Ben agreed. "But still—I mean,

somebody killed the guy, Reed. Somebody wanted to stop him from getting to you, so . . ."

"They killed him," Reed said. "But we don't really know why, do we?"

"No, but . . ."

"Trust me," Reed said, clapping Ben on the shoulder. "Nothing is going to go wrong here."

Famous last words, Ben thought, and tried to think of another way to phrase his concerns. He was still trying to think of one when a voice from behind him spoke.

"Doctor Richards, I hope you're going to rejoin us soon."

Ben turned around and found himself looking at a stocky man in his midforties—dark hair buzzed short, black turtleneck, wire-rim glasses, a very familiar face.

"Yates," Ben said.

"That's right." The man held out his hand. "Anthony Yates. You're Ben Grimm. A pleasure to finally make your acquaintance."

"Right," Ben said. "A pleasure."

Which was a lie—he didn't like Yates. Ten years earlier, when Reed had been looking for backing for the spacecraft he was building, Yates—fresh off his first billion dollars—had offered to supply it, on the condition that he also get to supply the crew for the ship. Reed had agreed, at first, but balked when Yates wanted to replace Ben with his own private pilot. The two had argued for quite a while before Reed finally decided to go elsewhere for funding. Ben had overheard that argument, had heard Yates give Reed an earful about how unqualified Ben Grimm was to fly his spacecraft—any spacecraft.

Ben took the man's hand ever so lightly. Yates squeezed back. The guy was surprisingly strong.

"Just finishing up here, Tony," Reed said. "Be with you in a minute."

"Good." Yates smiled and let go of Ben's hand, none the worse for wear. "I'm anxious to see how you've handled the decoherence effect."

"You'll see just that," Reed said. "In a minute."

Yates nodded. "In a minute, then." He bowed to Sue and Reed and excused himself.

Now Reed was frowning.

"What's the matter?" Sue asked.

Reed shook his head. "Not sure."

"Guy's a jerk, is what's the matter," Ben said. "Why'd you invite him?"

"I didn't. General Ross did. Most of the software the military runs is his. They want his take on whether or not it'll work with a quantum machine."

"Will it?"

Reed smiled. "He'll have some pretty major retooling to do."

"Couldn't happen to a nicer guy," Ben said. "So what's this decoherence effect he's talking about?"

"It has to do with the Q-bits. You'll see." He glanced over Ben's shoulder at the rest of the crowd.

"I'd better get back to it." Reed put a hand on Sue's shoulder and smiled.

She leaned up and kissed his cheek.

Ben watched his friend walk back through the crowd and frowned.

"Everything's going to be fine." Sue walked up next to him and spoke quietly. "Reed wouldn't go ahead with the demonstration if he wasn't a hundred percent certain that nothing would go wrong."

Ben nodded. "Sure. You're right, Suzy."

She smiled. "I'm always right. Ask Reed."

Ben smiled back. Sure she was. Old Stretch would never go ahead with anything that wasn't a hundred percent foolproof. Except . . .

There was that little experiment of his a few years back, the spaceship that Yates had tried to finance, the one Ben ended up piloting, with Sue and her brother Johnny along as passengers, the ship that had gone through the cosmic rays and come out untouched, which was more than you could say for the people inside—himself, of course, changed from Caucasian to orange rock, Reed from scientist to rubber band, Sue from cover girl to invisible girl, and Johnny . . .

Ben frowned. Come to think of it, where was the match head this morning?

"Thank you all for waiting," Reed said, stepping up next to the computer again. "Now—where was I?"

"About to give me my cipher," the general said.

"Exactly. Your cipher. Your unbreakable cipher—

one of the many things a working quantum computer could provide, like a complete map of my friend Ben's genome"—he tapped the picture on the display screen—"the accurate calcuation of any number of real-world probabilities. Unfortunately, as many of you know, the problem we've always faced in constructing a working quantum computer is overcoming the decoherence effect—the tendency of those Q-bits to decay before we can accurately assess their status."

"You want to put that into English?" the general asked.

"Before we can tell whether they're on or off, or somewhere in between," Yates put in. "Roughly speaking."

"Roughly speaking," Reed agreed. "Is that clearer, general?"

The older man shrugged. "Clear as it's going to get, I suppose. The things fall apart before you can measure them."

"Exactly. Over the last few months, in conjunction with some other work I've been doing, I believe I've discovered a way to prevent that from happening."

Reed stepped to the back of the stage then, took hold of the curtain there, and pulled it aside.

The general dropped the cigar from between his teeth.

Sitwell leaned forward and squinted.

People—Ben was too surprised to know whether he was one of them—gasped.

"Ladies, gentlemen," Reed said. "This is the Q-Ray."

They were all looking at another machine, one that dwarfed the box already up on the stage. This one looked like a cross between a telescope and a Kree blaster on steroids—a control panel of some kind, a long central barrel with a half dozen other smaller barrels hanging off it, all metal and sharp angles and powerful-looking.

Reed stepped around to the control panel and flicked a switch.

Lights flickered to life all over the machine. A low-frequency thrum sounded. Reed swung the main barrel around and pointed it at the quantum computer.

"It's going to take a few minutes to warm up," Reed said. "So while we wait, I'll explain exactly what it is we're going to see here today. *Q-Ray* is short for *quantum ray,* though the name is really a bit of a misnomer, as what the machine actually does is . . ."

"Create a Hilbert space," Yates interrupted.

Reed smiled. "Exactly. A stable, finite Hilbert space."

"A what?" the general said.

"A Hilbert space," Yates said. "Dr. Richards has been publishing a series of articles on such spaces recently. Mathematical dimensions called Hilbert spaces."

"You've been keeping tabs on me, Tony."

"Of course, Reed."

"I'm surprised. I would have thought theoretical

physics out of your area of expertise. A shade esoteric for you and your company."

"I'm always interested in what you're up to, Reed," Yates said. "No matter how esoteric."

"I'm flattered."

Sue leaned close and whispered to Ben. "You know, I never liked him."

"Yates?" Ben nodded. "I'm with you there."

"You two are talking about physics, right?" the general said. "Like string theory?"

"Not really like string theory, no," Reed said, and smiled.

Yates smiled, too, and Ben thought: *String theory. Strands.*

"The strands will come apart," Diehl said.

Ben frowned.

"Hey," he began, and stepped forward.

Sue touched him on the arm. "Ben," she said again. "Everything will be fine."

He nodded. Right. Fine. Everything was gonna be fine.

Except there was a little tingle at the back of his neck that said otherwise.

" 'Scuse me a minute," he said to Sue and Sitwell, and left them staring after him, puzzled expressions on their faces, as Reed continued his explanation of the Q-Ray.

Ben headed for the other side of the building, for the command center. Probably Sue was right, probably

Reed was right, probably Diehl didn't know anything about quantum physics. But . . .

He was going to check anyway.

The comm center was wall-to-wall computer screens, servers, databases. Ben logged on using the keyboard Reed had built him—about two times normal size—and found Flynn had been as good as his word; Diehl's file was waiting for him. He scrolled through it as quickly as he could.

Diehl had been caught stealing some artifacts out of the Rumanian embassy back in 1987. He'd claimed the artifacts were of great mystical significance; nothing further in the file about that. What was there was the man's penal record: Rikers for the last twenty years, the last decade in Building Twelve, which he'd shared with characters like Roustabout, Trapster, Diablo, Mad Thinker . . .

Ben frowned.

The Mad Thinker.

Name unknown. Genius type, mad scientist—hence the name—and an expert in computers.

Thinker and Diehl had done time together. Maybe they'd been buddies. Maybe Diehl had picked up a little computer know-how from the Thinker, maybe even learned a little quantum physics. Maybe.

On the other hand, Diehl had done time with a few hundred people in Building Twelve, not just the Thinker. The two of them hadn't necessarily known each other at all.

The strands will come apart.

He ought to tell Reed. He ought to tell Reed now, before . . .

Ben glanced up and to his right. On one of the screens, video feed was coming in from the lab; he found the audio that went with it and turned it up.

Reed and Yates were talking about Hilbert spaces.

". . . a tremendous energy drain," Yates said.

"Not prohibitive. A lot of the problem is software-based," Reed said. "Defining the characteristics of the space. The energy needed to create it then is a one-time burst."

"A very powerful burst, nonetheless," Yates said.

"Agreed," Reed said. "But I've utilized Laurico-Bates dampeners, so that . . ."

Everyone else in the room looked as if their eyes were glazing over. Ten seconds of listening to the two of them, Ben felt just the same. Hilbert spaces, blah blah blah.

He was being a worrywart. Nothing was going to happen here today.

But that little tingle of unease at the base of his spine wouldn't go away.

He turned the audio down and turned to Diehl's file again.

There wasn't much else to look at. The man had been a model prisoner, had done his time without a fuss, without ever raising any trouble. The last entry in the file was from Flynn, noting that since his release three weeks ago, Diehl had been neither seen nor heard from by anyone. Not until this morning, at least, when he'd shown up on a Manhattan-bound F and gotten himself killed by some kind of . . .

"Robot," Ben said out loud, and frowned.

The Mad Thinker built robots, too; usually really lifelike ones. Last Ben had heard, S.H.I.E.L.D. was after him to do some work for them on the LMDs they always used. Sitwell could probably fill him in on what was up with that now, though the important thing was that Thinker also built robots that were a little less humanoid-looking, ones that, now that he thought about it, sounded to him remarkably similar to that "monster" Olga had met on the F train this morning.

He shut Diehl's file and accessed what they had on the Thinker. A few file pictures going back to the first time they'd run into him, when old Willie Lumpkin had saved the day, a shot of Big Andy, Awesome Andy, without a doubt the ugliest android the Thinker had ever built—thing had a head like a big gray eraser, fifteen feet tall, fifteen hundred pounds . . .

"Going through the family photo album?"

Ben turned and saw Johnny Storm smiling at him.

Next to Johnny was one of the most beautiful women Ben had seen in a good long time; at least since last night, anyway, when he had taken Alicia to a chamber music concert. It had gone about as wrong as a date could go, which was neither here nor there at the moment, except that seeing Johnny with yet another gorgeous girl on his arm reminded Ben of all the things that he was never going to have, and never going to be.

Not that he would ever let the kid in on any of that.

"Har-har," Ben said. "Stick around a minute, I might need you."

He was pretty certain of that, in fact. The robots, and the fact that Diehl and Thinker were on the same cell block . . . one coincidence too many for him.

"Why? What's up?" Johnny asked.

"Not quite sure," he said. He turned to the woman. "You goin' to introduce me to your friend?"

"This is Amara Kenney," Johnny said. "She works with Yates."

"You have my sympathies," Ben said before he could stop himself.

The woman looked at him blankly.

"It's a joke," Ben said.

"A joke." Her expression didn't change.

"You know what a joke is?"

"Hey." Johnny stepped between him and Kenney. "What put you in such a mood?"

"Bad coffee," Ben said. "Talking rats."

"Huh?"

"Never mind. Listen," Ben said, suddenly serious. "I gotta go talk to Reed for a second. You stay here. Monitor the situation."

"Situation?" Johnny frowned, suddenly serious. "What situation?"

Ben opened his mouth to tell him—

And a faint chime sounded from the console behind him.

Ben turned. It was the phone—a call coming in from the security desk, from the building lobby downstairs.

He picked it up.

"Grimm."

"It's O'Hoolihan, sir. Wanted to let you know up there we got the cars running again. If you want to send down your elevator, I'll send them right up."

"Them?"

"Doctor Richards's guests. The computer people."

Ben got a sinking feeling in his stomach. He activated the lobby video feed. O'Hoolihan's face filled the screen. Two people stood behind him. One was Tony Yates. The other was Amara Kenney.

"Ben Grimm," Yates said, leaning forward, brushing dust off his black turtleneck. "We meet at last."

Ben said a four-letter word and turned to look at the screen showing the feed from the lab.

Yates had stepped up onto the stage next to Reed, only of course it wasn't Yates.

It was a duplicate. An android. The Mad Thinker, Jembay Diehl, the strands . . .

"Hey," Johnny said. "Amara. That girl on the screen—she looks just like . . ."

Ben heard a *whoof* and turned in time to see Johnny collapse on the floor.

The girl—the android—reached back and, before Ben could react, hit him, too.

"Oof," Ben said. He hadn't had time to brace himself; he went flying backward, out through the window and into the air.

He fell toward the ground, forty stories below.

3

BEN ROLLED AROUND IN MIDAIR, CUPPED HIS hands to his mouth, and shouted out: "INCOMING!"

People on the ground below looked up just in time to move out of the way.

He hit the sidewalk, went through the cement, and the ground underneath, and the roof of the subway station, and landed on the track with a loud thud.

He lay there a second, collecting his wits. Gathering his thoughts.

Getting ticked off.

One of these days, Ben told himself, people—by which he meant Reed and Sue, in that order—*are going to learn to listen to me when I tell 'em I have a funny feeling about something.*

He got to his feet.

Three transit cops looked down from the platform at him.

Flynn stood with them.

"What the—Ben?" He squinted. "What's happening? What is it?"

"What is it?" Ben looked up at the hole he'd made, back at the sky above, and frowned. If he was the Hulk, he'd jump right back through there, but he wasn't the Hulk. Quickest way back up for him was the way he'd come in half an hour ago, through the lobby and the elevator.

"It's clobberin' time, is what it is," he told Flynn, as he boosted himself up onto the platform, and started to run.

He ran straight up the metal divider between the escalator and the stairs, ignoring the shouts of people around him, he ran through the lobby of the Baxter Building, ignoring whatever it was Yates (the real Yates) and O'Hoolihan yelled after him, he ran into the express elevator, at which point he stood stock still for six point six seconds, smacking his fist into his palm.

Clobberin' time, he thought to himself. *Clobberin' time, clobberin' time, clobberin' time.*

It was what his brother always used to say, what he had used to psych Ben up before a gang fight, back when they were kids, back when they had to stand up for themselves and their friends, their right to walk around the neighborhood without getting the crap kicked out of them.

After Dan died, Ben had adopted it as his own personal mantra.

The elevator door opened.

Sitwell stood to Ben's left, fighting with a man in a business suit, who, of course, wasn't a man at all. He saw Sue surrounded by four men, two in business suits, two in turtlenecks just like Yates; he saw more businessmen fighting some of the military types; he saw two men in uniform down, a puddle of blood next to one of them, and he knew that the fight wasn't going so well there; and on the makeshift stage, right in front of the Q-Ray, he saw Reed going at it with Yates, who had suddenly sprouted a full head of hair, a very familiar, mad-scientist-looking head of hair, which was when Ben realized that though Amara Kenney and the rest of them were androids, Yates himself wasn't.

The man who'd come in here masquerading as Tony Yates was in fact the Mad Thinker himself, and that made him the most dangerous one out of all of them.

Ben saw all this in a few seconds—how many exactly he didn't know for sure, but definitely less than six point six—and then he moved.

He grabbed one of the androids bothering Sue by the shoulder and spun it around.

The thing reared back to clock him, only Ben was ready, and when its arm shot forward, he stopped the blow with an outstretched palm and then gathered the android's hand in that palm and grabbed it, and squeezed, and heard something crunch, and the thing tried to pull away and Ben held on to the arm, and reared back with his right leg, and kicked out, and then the thing and its arm were suddenly—

Separated.

The android frowned. Ben whacked it across the face with its own arm, and it fell to the ground, sparking and convulsing.

"Ben!" he heard Sue shout, and turned in time to see another android in a suit coming at him, and he whacked that one with the arm, too. Half the skin on its face came off, revealing smooth metal. Ben hit it again—this time, *it* was ready and grabbed the arm, and the arm snapped. Somebody jumped on him from behind and pinned his arms for a second. The android hit him with the half an arm it was holding, once, and then again and again and again, too fast for Ben to follow. His vision swam.

The android in front of him burst into flame. It burned for half a second, then collapsed to the floor, all burning, sparking circuits.

Johnny, standing right behind it, gave him the thumbs-up.

Ben drove backward, slamming the android holding his arms into the wall. Its grip loosened. Ben freed one arm, reached over his head, and flipped the thing over onto the ground in front of him. It looked up, he jumped down, landing on it with both feet, hard as he could, caving in its chest with a crunch.

The head looked up at him.

"Disassociation," it said. "Termination."

"You got that right," Ben said, and turned toward the stage, just as Reed landed on the ground next to him.

"Stop him," Reed said, and coughed. He reached up and put a hand on Ben's arm. "He's going to use the Q-Ray; I don't know what his plans are, but . . ."

Reed's eyes widened. Ben turned just in time to see Johnny fly backward and slam into the wall behind them.

The Torch let fly with a string of curses and put a hand to the back of his head.

On the stage, Yates—the Thinker—lowered his hand. He had something that looked like a laser pointer in it, only Ben didn't think the little red glow coming off the top of it was as harmless as the things you bought at Staples.

"Easy, Stretch," Ben said. "I'll get him."

"Ben." Reed coughed again. "Don't. It's a neuralyzer of some sort, it will . . ."

He ignored his friend and started toward the stage.

Clobberin' time, clobberin' time, clobberin' time.

Amara Kenney—the robot one, Ben could tell because the skin, or plastic, or whatever it was, was worn off on one hand, probably from hitting him before—stepped into his path.

Ben grabbed her by the throat with one hand and walked on, dragging her along with him, squeezing as he went, loosening his grip a little when she stopped making noises.

Yates—the Thinker—looked up as Ben approached the stage. "Your turn," he said, and raised the thing that looked like a pen.

Ben threw the Kenney android at him. The Thinker dodged, but not quite quickly enough. Part of the android caught his arm, and the pen thing went skittering across the floor.

The general, hiding underneath one of the chairs, picked it up and got to his feet.

"Step away from that machine, Yates," the older man said. "You're done here."

The Thinker shook his head. "I'm not Yates. And I'd be careful with that if I were you, it's actually quite . . ."

There was a sudden flash of light, so bright Ben had to shield his eyes.

". . . sensitive," the Thinker finished.

Ben blinked and looked where the general had stood, only the general wasn't there anymore.

"Not very good at taking orders, was he?" The Thinker smiled at Ben.

"Let's see if you're any better," Ben said, starting toward him. "Get away from Reed's gizmo, and I won't break you in two. Not right away, at least."

"I don't think I will, actually," the Thinker said, and reached into his pocket and pulled out another one of his little pens. "I calculated a thirty-eight-point-six-percent chance I would need a second one of these, and so—"

Ben lunged at him.

The Thinker raised the pen. Blue fire shot through the air.

Ben lost control of his limbs and fell to the ground.

He lost control of everything for a minute; the world went herky-jerky on him, he still had a vague idea of where he was, he heard gunfire and fighting and screams, but he couldn't make sense of any of it. His arms were shaking, and he couldn't stop them. His eyes were blinking, and he couldn't stop them, either.

His head was banging up and down on the floor. He heard the Thinker laughing.

Time—a few seconds, a few minutes, Ben didn't know for sure—passed.

Ben opened his eyes.

He was lying half on, half off the stage.

The Thinker was standing next to the Q-Ray. Sprawled on the ground in front of him was Sitwell, and young Jasper did not look good.

Young Jasper's neck was bent at a funny angle.

Young Jasper looked dead.

The Thinker was talking.

". . . because they're just equations. And you know what the lovely thing about equations is?"

Ben heard coughing, and then: "Listen to me. You don't know what you're doing."

That was Reed's voice. Ben managed to turn his head just enough to see that two of the Thinker's androids were holding Stretch up between them, propping him up was more like it, forcing him to watch—and listen to—what their master was doing.

"The lovely thing about equations," the Thinker continued, ignoring Reed, "is that you can rewrite them. Which I've just finished doing. Which means your Hilbert space is now my Hilbert space. A much bigger Hilbert space. An exclusionary Hilbert space."

"I didn't build the machine to work that way," Reed said. "To generate that kind of power."

"No, you didn't. Which is why it's taking me so long to reconfigure the—ah." He smiled and stepped back from the controls. "That ought to do it."

Reed twisted in the androids' grasp. "You'll blow us all to kingdom come."

"Admittedly, there's a fifteen-point-six-percent chance you're right," the Thinker said. "But those are odds I'm willing to take."

Clobberin' time, Ben thought. *Clobberin' time, clobberin' time, clobberin' time.*

He grunted.

The Thinker's head swiveled around.

"Well. Look who's back with us—more or less," he said.

"Laugh while you can, you big monkey," Ben said,

or tried to say, only what came out was more like a long, continuous moan, with his teeth chattering during half of it.

The Thinker smiled and turned away.

"Because if I'm right," he continued, walking to the far side of the machine, "in a few seconds, I'm going to have a rare opportunity indeed. The chance to stand within that space and reshape it."

He leaned down and flipped open a panel. Metal struck metal, made a little clinking sound.

"In a way, it'll be like creating the universe. Recreating the universe, really, only according to my own particular little plan. Which I suppose makes me God—or something akin to it."

Ben didn't like the sound of that.

Clobberin' time, he thought. *Clobberin' time, clobberin' time, clobberin' time,* and willed his legs to stop shaking.

But they didn't.

Damn it. Where the hell was Johnny? And Sue? And S.H.I.E.L.D., for God's sake, you'd think Sitwell would have sent for reinforcements or something, you'd think maybe one of the Avenjerks would be monitoring the emergency channel, you'd think somebody, somewhere, would be on their way, because . . .

The Thinker slapped a button. The low-pitched thrum the Q-Ray was making, had been making since Reed first turned it on, suddenly trebled in intensity.

Reed twisted and cried out in frustration.

Maybe it was Ben's imagination, maybe it was the aftereffects of whatever it was the Thinker had zapped him with, but all at once, he thought he saw the Q-Ray gizmo giving off a faint golden glow.

"You're mad," Reed said.

"That's what they call me," the Thinker agreed. "Ever since I was a little boy, that's what they called me."

The glow increased.

Clobberin' time, Ben told himself. *Clobberin' time, clobberin' time, clobberin' time,* and he clamped one hand to his side and held it there.

The shaking began to subside.

"Nobody used my name. Not then, not now, not ever. But it doesn't matter anymore." The Thinker put a hand on the Q-Ray. The glow enveloped him.

"Goodbye, Richards," he said. "I don't expect that there'll be a place for you in the new world I'm creating, I'm afraid. Not for you, or any of your associates."

A little chill ran down Ben's spine.

No place for Reed, or any of his associates. Which meant him, and Johnny, and Sue, and . . .

Alicia.

Ben gritted his teeth.

And somehow got to his feet.

The Thinker's eyes widened in surprise.

"Clobberin' time," Ben managed, and drew back his arm to strike.

He stumbled and fell forward. His hand hit the machine.

The glow got brighter.

He grabbed the Thinker's arm. The Thinker's eyes widened, and he shouted something, and . . .

Interlude one

THE GLOW ATE HIM, AND THE GLOW DISAPPEARED.

That's what it felt like to Ben. One second, he was in the middle of this bright light, and the next, the light was gone, and everywhere Ben looked—up, down, left, right—there was blackness.

He couldn't see his hands in front of his face, he couldn't see his feet, he couldn't see the Thinker, or Reed's machine, or Reed, or the Baxter Building . . .

"Reed?" he said. "Suzy? Where is everybody?"

No sound came out of his mouth.

"Reed?" he said again, and took a step forward.

Only he didn't move.

Which was when Ben realized that not only

couldn't he see his feet, he couldn't feel them. *Oh, man,* he thought, reaching his hands to his face, only he didn't have those, either.

He didn't have a body at all.

What had he done? What had the Thinker done?

Ben started yelling. He yelled for a while, yelled without making a sound until he remembered something important.

Hilbert space. Thinker said he was going to make a Hilbert space, whatever the heck that was. From the way he and Reed had been talking about it, it was one of those sort of alternate dimensions Reed was always exploring, and so . . . that's where Ben was. A Hilbert space. Just realizing that made him feel better—you had to define a problem before you could solve it, that was what Reed was always saying, and now he'd defined it, so the problem was getting out of here, and back to reality.

Right then, Ben heard something. A noise. A kid crying. He turned—well, not exactly turned, since he didn't really have a body at this point, it was more like he spun the blackness around him, until he saw a little pinprick of light. He spun everything again, and the pinprick became kind of like the head of a needle. There was a face in it. The kid's face. The kid who was crying.

The kid was Reed—a superskinny, supergeeky Reed, but Ben still recognized him right away. Reed was in a bathroom someplace, looked like a school, and a bunch of other kids were calling him names, making fun of him.

"Smart mouth!" they shouted.

"Swirly!" they cried, and stuffed his head in a toilet.

"Stop it," a voice said, and Ben spun the world again and saw . . .

Himself. Standing in the bathroom door, wearing a letter jacket, only Ben never had a letter jacket in his life.

And he hadn't known Reed until he went to Empire State University.

What was he looking at, anyway?

"I'm sorry to find you so set against me, Ben," and that was Reed's voice, too, an older Reed, and Ben spun things around again to see . . .

Himself, and Reed, and Sue, and Johnny, the night they'd decided to fly Reed's spaceship themselves and not wait for the government to give them permission.

Or rather, Reed had decided, and Ben had gone along.

Here they were now, just as they had been ten years ago . . .

Reed took a pipe out of his mouth and shook his head.

Ben frowned.

Reed? A pipe?

"I never thought you would be a coward," Sue said.

Ben watched himself slam his fist down on the table.

These next words, the words he was about to speak, he knew by heart.

"A coward? Nobody calls me a coward. Get me that plane. I'll fly her."

Except before he could say them, Reed stepped forward.

"Ben—you're right, of course. It would be madness to risk our lives like this. We'll wait."

"Now you're talking sense," the Ben in front of him said, and smiled.

Hilbert space. *Crazy place,* Ben thought, and spun all around.

There were little points of light everywhere, he realized that now, and inside those points of light . . .

Faces. He spun the world around to see them better, and then he realized something else.

They weren't points of light, they were more like little strings, a lot of the points all connected, scenes happening alongside one another, like cut-up pieces of filmstrips.

Like strands.

The strands will come apart.

What in Sam Hill was going on here?

And then a voice he hadn't heard for years, a voice he'd never thought to hear again, sounded behind him, and he spun, and saw . . .

Dan.

His big brother.

"You take one, too, Benjy," Dan said, a teenage

Dan, and Ben was a teenager, too, a couple of years younger, and he held out his hand, and into it Dan put . . .

A gun.

And they walked down Yancy Street, the block between McGraw and Stanton, guns tucked into the waistbands of their pants, and there was a bunch of kids waiting on the corner of McGraw for them, and Dan walked up and shot one, and the cops came and took him away, and there was a trial, guilty, guilty, guilty, they put Dan in an injection chamber, they tied him down, they shot him full of poison.

Ben and Aunt Penny and Uncle Jake stood over the coffin.

"You take one, too, Benjy," Dan said. Ben heard him again, and spun the world, and there he was, another set of lights, another strand, another teenage Dan, handing another teenage Ben a gun, and they opened the door to the apartment and stepped out into the stairwell, and . . .

Clack-clack, clack-clack, clack-clack.

Gunfire.

Two kids wearing red kerchiefs, standing on the floor above them. Screams.

Aunt Penny and Uncle Jake standing over two coffins.

"No, Benjy," Dan said, and Ben spun the world again, and there he was, watching the apartment door close behind his big brother, running to the window, seeing Dan walk that block between McGraw and Stanton, this was how it had really happened, here came the other kids and Dan walking straight on to meet them, and then . . .

Ambush. Dan getting shot, Ben screaming, Ben and Aunt Penny and Uncle Jake standing over the coffin and . . .

"Your name is Max, isn't it?"

That was a voice he didn't recognize. Ben spun the world again, and there was the Thinker.

He was standing in the middle of a whole lot of strands, thin ones that seemed to be peeling off from one another, like threads fraying off a rope. He reached out with a hand and touched one of those strands closest to him.

There was an expression on his face that Ben had never seen before.

Sadness.

"It's you," he whispered. "Rose. I forgot about you, how could I forget . . ."

The Thinker pulled the strand toward him.

And the world spun, and this time, Ben spun with it, spun around, and around and around and when he opened his eyes . . .

He was right in front of the Thinker.

And the Thinker was huge.

A thousand, ten thousand feet tall, so big that Ben was a speck against him, so big that all Ben could see of the man was his face, and not even all of that, just the eyes, the bridge of the nose, enough to recognize him.

Ben looked into those eyes and saw a scene reflected there. From one of the strands, he realized. Inside it, a girl was talking.

"Max," she said. "Why are you so angry?"

She couldn't have been more than seven. A little boy stood next to her. Hard to tell for sure, but Ben thought he looked like the Thinker might have looked as a kid.

"Don't be angry, Max," the girl said, only now she wasn't a girl anymore, she was a teenager.

And the Thinker was a teenager, too. And he and the girl were walking in snow somewhere, hand in hand, but . . .

The Thinker was also there, in front of Ben, sad, and pulling on the one strand in the blackness, pulling it closer and closer, and the reflection in his eyes grew bigger as he pulled, and the scenes started to fly past, changing from the Thinker and the girl to a new scene, and then another, and another and another and another, and as the scenes flew past, so, too, did faces, some he didn't recognize, some he did, there was Johnny and Sue, and Reed, and Alicia, and the waitress from downstairs, Olga, and Doom, of course, Doom, Doom was everywhere, and there was Yates, or rather the Thinker pretending to be Yates, in the lab, seated in front of the Q-Ray, and the reflection drew closer and closer and got somehow less like a reflection and more like reality.

Another strand flew past, and there was the girl again, and the Thinker, and Yates, and then another strand, the Thinker and the girl walking in snow, and then another, and another, and Ben heard the Thinker saying, "Yes, yes," and then he saw Yates again, and the Baxter Building, and there was Diehl.

Jembay Diehl, alive again, and standing next to the Q-Ray, a puzzled expression on his face.

"This is wrong," he said. "This is not how it's supposed to be."

"The source of your confusion escapes me," came another voice. "However, you are undeniably correct; this is not how it's supposed to be, as you do not belong here in our headquarters."

And the Mad Thinker, dressed in a black-and-white Fantastic Four uniform, stepped up onto the demonstration stage next to Diehl, and suddenly, it all seemed wrong to Ben, too.

But then that second passed.

Clobberin' time, he thought, and stepped up onto the stage as well.

4

THE MAN RAISED HIS HANDS TO DEFEND HIMSELF, but Ben was already swinging.

Something made him hold his punch at the last second, though. Instead of the haymaker he'd meant to land on the man's jaw, he grazed him with little more than a love tap.

The man flew across the stage and landed hard against the wall.

The confusion in his eyes changed to anger.

The man lifted a hand, and a globe of red light formed in the air before him.

It hovered for a second and then shot forward as if it had been spit out of a cannon.

It hit Ben like a cannonball, too, square in the gut, no longer just light but solid as a rock.

It hit him, and it exploded at the same instant. It had a kick like a dozen hand grenades, though, of course, it wasn't science at all, it was obviously sorcery, which made this guy, whoever he was, some kind of sorcerer, too.

Ben had the man's name on the tip of his tongue for a second, but then the second was gone, and the blast and the impact catapulted him backward.

He smashed into a window, and then through it, plummeting toward the street below.

In midair, he managed to turn around, cup his hands to his mouth, and shout out: "INCOMING!"

People on the ground below looked up just in time to move out of the way.

He hit the sidewalk, went through the cement, and the ground underneath, and the roof of the subway station, and landed on the track with a loud thud.

He lay there a second, collecting his wits. Gathering his thoughts.

He had the strangest feeling of déjà vu.

He shook it off and rushed into the Baxter Building.

Clobberin' time, he thought to himself as the elevator shot up toward the lab.

It was what his brother always used to say, though he doubted Dan said it much anymore, down on Wall Street—but Ben still did. It was his own personal mantra now.

The elevator door opened. For a second, Ben was confused all over again.

The androids were fighting their guests. The FF's androids, a half dozen of them, were going at it with the army and S.H.I.E.L.D. personnel that had come for this morning's demonstration of the quantum computer. Ben counted two of the Roberta models, the ones they used for office work, three of the O'Hoolihans, who did security, and one of the maintenance droids, an older Simek model. The Robertas and the Simek were fighting the army men, who'd formed themselves into a rough circle around General Ross with weapons drawn, the O'Hoolihans were going at it with Sitwell and the others from S.H.I.E.L.D.

Up on the demonstration stage, the sorcerer guy was walking all around the Q-Ray, which was surrounded by some kind of energy field. He looked angry. He looked frustrated.

He looked, all at once, somehow familiar.

He was black, maybe late thirties, early forties, big guy, powerfully built, that jailhouse lifting-weights, pumped-up kind of build. A criminal, obviously, but Ben couldn't place the man's name for some reason, and he was usually pretty good about names.

"Ben."

He turned his head left and saw Max getting to his feet. His uniform was torn on one shoulder.

His Fantastic Four uniform.

The Thinker, Ben thought, *was wearing a Fantastic Four uniform.*

For a second, that looked strange to Ben. Wrong. Then that second passed, and suddenly what seemed strange was that he was thinking of the man alongside him as the Thinker, which was what the press always called him, instead of Max. His good friend Max. His comrade-in-arms for the past ten years.

"What's going on here?" Ben asked.

"Our guest has turned the help against us," Max said, pointing toward the sorcerer.

"The androids."

"Exactly."

"Who is he?"

"Undetermined."

"What's he want?"

"The Q-Ray, I surmise. I have activated a protective force screen, which for the moment is denying him access to it."

"Where's Reed?"

"I have been unable to establish communication with the inner lab. I have summoned the Torch, however."

"The Torch." Ben shook his head. "Don't talk to me about the Torch," he said, and then, having established the good guys and bad guys in his mind, waded into the fray.

One of the O'Hoolihans was closest, fighting three of the S.H.I.E.L.D. agents, including Sitwell. Ben grabbed the android by the shoulder and spun it around.

The thing reared back to clock him, only Ben was ready, and when its arm shot forward, Ben caught it and held, reared back with his right leg, and kicked out, and then the thing and its arm were suddenly . . .

Separated.

The O'Hoolihan frowned. Ben whacked it across the face with its own arm, and it fell to the ground, sparking and convulsing.

"Mister Grimm!" he heard Sitwell shout, and turned in time to see a second O'Hoolihan coming at him, and he whacked that one with the arm, too. Half the skin on its face came off, revealing smooth metal. Ben hit it again—this time, *it* was ready and grabbed the arm, and the arm snapped. Somebody—Ben caught a glimpse of blond hair, one of the Robertas, he guessed—jumped on him from behind and pinned his arms for a second. The O'Hoolihan hit him with the half an arm it was holding, once, and then again and again and again, too fast for Ben to follow. His vision swam.

The Roberta holding him relaxed its grip.

The O'Hoolihan in front of him stopped moving.

He shoved backward, and the Roberta toppled to the floor with a crash.

Max stood in front of him, smiling, holding a control panel in his hands.

"I recompiled the movement subroutines, deleting those related to gross motor function."

"You mean you hit the off switch," Ben said.

"There is no off switch. I didn't design them with off switches."

"Woulda been a lot easier, don't you think?" Ben asked, stepping over the O'Hoolihan as he started forward, toward the stage, where the sorcerer was trying to break through the force screen around the Q-Ray.

"Hey!" Ben yelled. "Whoever you are, whatever you're doing here, you better . . ."

The sorcerer turned and waved a hand—green fire crackled in the air and shot toward Ben. He threw himself to one side just in time—the bolt of energy went past harmlessly.

The old football reflexes, Ben thought with satisfaction. Good to know he still had 'em.

He heard a noise like a grunt behind him and turned in time to see the O'Hoolihan on the ground suddenly open its eyes and sit up.

Ben jumped down on the android, landing on it with both feet, hard as he could, caving in its chest with a crunch.

The O'Hoolihan looked up at him.

"Disassociation," it said. "Termination."

Déjà vu, Ben thought, as the android closed its eyes.

Déjà vu? Why?

He shrugged the feeling off and turned to Max.

"Off switches," his friend said. "You may have something there, Ben."

That was one android down, and it took Ben and

the army officers and the S.H.I.E.L.D. agents a good three more minutes to finish off the other five. As Ben fought, he kept one eye on the sorcerer, who was still trying to force his way through the force screen around the Q-ray.

The last O'Hoolihan went down. Ben turned to Max, who was looking down at the control panel in his hand and frowning.

"Force-shield integrity is down to twenty percent." Max shook his head. "Sixty-two point six seconds before it fails, on my mark. Mark."

Ben nodded. About a minute. Well, this guy—whoever he was—wasn't going to get that minute. His time was up now.

Ben stepped onto the stage.

The sorcerer turned.

"Stay back," he said. "I don't want to hurt you."

"Right. I get that." Ben advanced. "That's why the androids. To protect me."

"You don't understand," the man said. "I want to protect you. I want to protect all of us. The machine has to be destroyed—before he can use it."

He pointed at Max as he spoke.

Ben and his friend both frowned. They exchanged a quick glance. They'd worked together long enough to give that glance specific meaning.

You take it, Ben said silently.

Max stepped up next to him.

"Sir. I assure you, my use of both Q-Ray and

quantum computer will not in any way threaten anyone, or anything."

The man shook his head. "You're wrong. You see, I remember now, so it's two of us who remember. Two of us. The strands come apart, and YOU"—he raised his voice suddenly—"YOU'RE RESPONSIBLE!"

The guy's eyes were wide as saucers. *He was nuts*, Ben realized. Certifiable. *No sense talking to him—should've clocked him before, when I had the chance.*

He wouldn't make that mistake again.

"That's why I have to destroy it," the man said. "It has to be destroyed. So you don't."

"If you could elaborate," Max said. "So I don't what?"

The sorcerer turned toward Max, opened his mouth to respond.

Ben launched himself forward, flying through the air toward the man, drawing his arm back to strike.

Sweet dreams, buddy, he thought, as his fist shot forward.

The sorcerer raised one hand, and blue fire, sparkling and crackling with energy, shot out of it.

His fist an inch away from its target, Ben's arm froze in midair.

So did the rest of him.

He hovered off the ground, paralyzed.

"So I don't what?" Max repeated. "Tell me what the danger is, and perhaps I can avoid it."

"YOU KNOW!" The sorcerer stepped forward, past Ben. He couldn't even move his eyes to follow.

"The strands," the man continued. "The strands come apart, and it's your fault."

"I assure you, I'll be very careful with the strands," Max said.

"DON'T TALK TO ME THAT WAY!" The sorcerer's voice moved farther away from him. "I'm not a crazy person. I'm the only one who understands. I'm the only one who knows."

Gunfire exploded.

Almost simultaneously, Ben heard the crackle of energy in the air again, the same sound that the sorcerer's attack on him had made, and a man—not Max—screamed.

Dammit, Ben thought, and tried to move, and failed.

Another man screamed.

"Stop!" Max yelled. "No more. Sir—if I am the problem, talk to me. Hurt me, not those men. If you tell me what the danger is with the Q-Ray, if you tell me a reason not to use it, I promise you I will not use it, I will not . . ."

"You've done it already, haven't you? Or have you—I can't take that chance," the man said, and energy crackled again, and this time it was Max who screamed.

Ben tried to move again, and couldn't. *Magic*, he thought. He hated magic, hated magicians, all of 'em, every last one, none of them fought fair, Doom and this guy whoever he was and Diablo and that Impossible Man clown and . . ."

Doc Strange, he thought. What was it Doctor Strange had told Ben when he'd come to help redesign the system? What was it Ben was supposed to keep in mind when fighting magic and not science?

Willpower, that was it.

Willpower was what magic worked on. Willpower was what would work against it. When Strange was here, after Doctor Doom's last attack, helping Reed and Max incorporate protection against eldritch energies into the Baxter Building's defenses, he'd showed them.

He'd made a rope out of energy and lassoed Ben with it. To get out, the man had said, all you need to do is concentrate. Concentrate, he'd told Ben.

Ben concentrated.

He stared at his fist frozen in the air in front of him and willed his fingers to move.

The sorcerer stepped into his field of vision and renewed his attack on the force shield protecting the Q-Ray. The glow around the machine began to dim visibly.

A minute, give or take a few seconds, Ben thought. That's what he had before the shield failed and this guy destroyed the machine. He had absolutely no idea what sort of craziness had taken hold of the man's mind that made him think the Q-Ray was dangerous—as far as Ben understood things, it was just some sort of gadget to help the quantum computer run better, but that was out of his field of expertise, and anyway, the point was that nobody, no one, not now, not ever, walked into the Baxter Building and started destroying stuff.

He concentrated, and his pinkie finger began to unclench.

"Stop."

That was Max again. From right behind him. He didn't sound good.

Take it easy, Max, Ben said silently in his mind. *Give me a second, I'll handle this.*

The sorcerer turned quickly and looked at Ben.

"I don't think you will," he said, which was when Ben realized he'd spoken out loud, that he could move his mouth, at least, and talk.

Almost, he thought. *A few seconds more, that's all I need.*

The sorcerer turned back to the force shield.

"Stop," Max said again, and Ben heard him shuffling forward, and then a second later saw movement out of the corner of his eye.

Max was hurt. Max was bleeding—badly. On the right side of his uniform, a patch the size of a basketball was wet with blood.

"I feel compelled to point out that destroying this machine will simply result in an inconvenience. We'll build another," Max said. "It's quite simple. The plans . . ."

The force shield blinked out of existence.

"The threat is now," the man said. "This instant, this machine. The rest doesn't matter."

Now, Ben thought. *Now or never.*

He took a halting step forward.

He fell face-first onto the ground.

"Ooof," he managed.

The sorcerer raised his arms over his head. His lips began to move.

"No," Max said.

"Yes," the man answered, and Ben could feel the energy gather around him.

Clobberin' time, he thought. *Clobberin' time, clobberin' time, clobberin' time.*

But he couldn't get up.

He'd failed, Ben thought, and again, he had the strangest sense of déjà vu.

Then glass exploded.

Fire flew through the room toward him, and then past, a heat so intense the breath rushed from his lungs for a second.

The flame hit the sorcerer head-on, and he screamed and flew backward through the air.

He crashed into the wall and lay still.

The flame landed in front of Ben, and went out.

Tony Yates—a.k.a. the Human Torch—looked down at Ben and shook his head.

"Fancy footwork there."

"Where were you?" Ben asked.

"Busy," Yates said, and then walked over to Max. "You all right?"

Max nodded. "No serious injuries. I believe, however, I will need point six seven pints of blood, transfused as quickly as possible."

"Point six seven," Yates said. "We'll get on it."

"Good," Max said, and managed a weak smile.

Ben frowned. Max looked pale—even paler than usual, which was saying something.

"You sure you're all right?" Ben asked.

"Absolutely," Max said. "Never better."

He closed his eyes then, and fainted.

Five minutes on, one of the Robertas was transfusing Max, who was conscious again, apparently none the worse for wear. He had his handy little control pad out on his lap and was using it to direct the cleanup, sending instructions to a room full of O'Hoolihans, Simeks, and Robertas, who were busy carting away and crushing the wreckage from the battle.

The sorcerer was still out cold. His uniform and his skin were badly burned along one side. Medi-bots were attending to him, too. He was a lot worse off than Max.

Odds were, he was dying.

Ben looked over at the Torch and shook his head. Ever since Elizabeth—and what was that, almost two months ago now?—the guy was dangerous. Ben had talked to him, Reed had talked to him, Max had talked to him, and yet . . .

"So we don't know who he is?" the Torch—Yates—asked again.

"Not a clue," Ben said. "I hope we'll be able to question him once he wakes up. If he wakes up."

Yates spun around.

"Next time," he said, glaring at Ben, "I suppose I'll just let him blow up whatever he wants."

"That's a helpful attitude," Ben shot back.

"Will somebody please tell me what in Sam Hill just happened here? Who was that lunatic? Where did he come from? Why was he trying to destroy that machine?" General Ross—who, once the sorcerer went down, had appeared out from behind a gaggle of bodyguards and started yelling—shoved himself between Ben and Yates and stared daggers at the two of them. "And where is Reed Richards?"

"Not here, obviously," Yates said.

"Hmmphhh." Ross snorted, and looked toward the far end of the room, toward the door to Reed's inner lab.

Ben and Max shared a glance.

Reed was in there, of course. For him not to show up for the demonstration was one thing, Max could handle the demonstration, but not to come out when things went to kingdom come . . .

Not a good sign, Ben thought. Something was going on in there, something bad, and Ben had the uncomfortable feeling he knew exactly what.

"We'll find him for you shortly, General," Max said. "In the meantime . . ."

"Excuse me."

Ben looked up and saw Sitwell standing over them.

"I believe I have identified the intruder."

Ben raised an eyebrow. "Oh?"

"Yes." Sitwell held up what looked like a cell phone with a slightly oversized screen. There was a picture on it.

Ben leaned forward.

The picture looked exactly like a younger version of the sorcerer.

"The screen is from a classified S.H.I.E.L.D. database containing the names of more than seven thousand individuals recently identified as 'persons of interest' in the ongoing Elizabeth investigation," Sitwell said. "This particular individual was released from Building Twelve on Rikers Island approximately three weeks ago, and . . ."

"Here. Let me see that." Ross shoved in between Ben and Sitwell and pushed his face right up against the little screen.

"That looks like him, all right," the general said an instant later. "Building Twelve, you said. So he's some kind of supervillain?"

Sitwell nodded. "Yes." He pressed a button on the side of the unit. The image disappeared, and text filled the screen.

"Jembay Diehl," Sitwell said. "A.k.a. Hoodoo Guru, a.k.a. Black Hand, captured November 3, 1985, at the Rumanian Embassy and sentenced to . . ."

"Diehl. That's it." Max looked up, as the medi-bot pulled a line out of his arm. "He was on the report Flynn gave us last week—remember, Ben?"

Ben nodded. That was why the guy looked so familiar. Flynn's report on ex-cons at large, whereabouts unknown—Diehl's picture had been on it. All the details came flooding back to him now—the guy getting caught at the embassy, getting twenty years, getting out, and disappearing into thin air, until today. Till he showed up here.

He frowned all at once.

That picture suddenly seemed incomplete. *There was something else about Diehl,* Ben thought. *Something he was forgetting.*

What?

"Puzzling," Max said.

Ben looked at him.

"You feel it, too?" he said.

"Feel what?" Max said, standing up.

"Whoa," Ben said. "You sure that's a good idea. Walking?"

Max nodded. "I've been given a combination of drugs to minimize pain and speed the healing process. I should be able to function at near optimum levels for the next three or four hours, until I can rest."

"Yeah, but . . ."

"What's puzzling?" Sitwell asked.

"The profile Mister Flynn gave us regarding this man," Max said. "The powers just demonstrated here dwarf those Diehl was supposedly capable of."

"Say that again," Ross put in.

"He's a lot more powerful than we were told," Ben explained.

"Than this says." Sitwell held up the device.

"How's that possible?" Ross asked.

"That's what we need to find out," Max said.

"Truth serum." Yates folded his arms across his chest. "You know where Reed keeps it—right, Max?"

"I do. But we need to stabilize his condition before we use something like that."

"Let's worry about his condition later. Let's get the answers now."

In response, Max looked down at the control pad in his hand.

"He has second-degree burns on a significant portion of his upper chest. He has third-degree burns on his right arm. The serum will not function optimally under those conditions. It may even cause further damage."

"That'd be a shame, hey?" Yates said.

Ben was getting a little tired of the Torch's attitude.

"It's not your decision to make, buddy," he said. "This is a team, in case you hadn't noticed, and we . . ."

"Team?" Yates snorted. "Hah."

Ben felt his fingers clench into a fist.

"Gentlemen." Max stepped between them. "My best guess, Mister Diehl will be unconscious another few hours. I suggest we treat him medically, secure him physically, and then . . ."

Across the room, someone screamed at the top of their lungs.

Ben looked and saw Diehl climbing to his feet. He had a medi-bot hanging off each arm, hooked up to him with IVs.

Yates burst into flame.

"Another few hours, huh?" he said, starting toward the man. "Looks like your calculations were off a little bit, Max."

"I don't see how. The man should not be conscious." Max frowned and looked up then, and saw Yates heading for Diehl. "Tony . . . don't do anything rash."

"I just want to make sure he doesn't get away," Yates said. "That's all."

He cupped his hand against his side, and suddenly, he was holding a ball of flame.

"Yates," Ben said, and at that instant Diehl screamed again, nonsense syllables, something wordless and inarticulate. A cry of pain, clearly.

The man looked, to Ben's eye, to be stretching. Getting longer, just the way Reed did, only in this case, the process did not look comfortable.

"Very strange," Max said. "Energy readings off the scale."

Diehl looked, literally, as if he were being pulled apart.

He screamed again and, a millisecond later, simply disappeared.

The medi-bots hanging off him fell to the floor with a loud clatter.

"Hmmm," Max said.

Yates cursed and flamed off.

"Would somebody mind telling me what just happened?" Ross asked.

"Guy magicked himself out of here, that's what just happened," Ben said, which shouldn't have been possible, not after the energy barriers Strange had helped them put around the building.

"I need to go to the lab," Max announced. "I want a real-time record of what just happened here."

"And I want to see Richards," General Ross repeated. "I took the red-eye in from San Modesto to see this quantum computer of his, and I'll be damned if I'm leaving before . . ."

"I know he wants to see you, too, General," Max interrupted. "But obviously, this is not the time. We need to restore order here. Figure out exactly what just happened. In the meantime—" He keyed in a series of commands on the control pad, and two of the Robertas appeared on either side of the general and his people.

"—I suggest you return to wherever it is you're staying. We'll call as soon as possible."

"We can show you the way out, gentlemen," the Robertas said simultaneously. "It would be our pleasure."

"Get these damn machines away from me." Ross turned and pointed his cigar at Max. "You oughtta scrap those things before they turn on you again."

"We're putting off switches on them next model revision," Ben said. "How's that sound?"

Ross glared and bit deeper into his cigar.

Sitwell stepped forward.

"This may actually be very fortuitous timing, General. Colonel Fury had asked me to seize a moment of your time if I could while you were in town."

Ross raised an eyebrow. "Oh?"

"Yes, sir. Pursuant to the Elizabeth investigation, we've gotten in some recon photos from the other side of the Iron Curtain. We could use an experienced eye in going over them."

The general harrumphed.

"Well," he finally said. "Always happy to help out the colonel."

Sitwell smiled.

The Robertas led the two contingents of men—S.H.I.E.L.D. and army—to the elevator. The doors opened and closed.

And then it was just the three of them—Ben, Max, and Yates—standing in the wreckage of the lab.

Three, supposed to be four, Ben thought, and looked again toward the door of Reed's lab.

"He's gone in, hasn't he?" Yates said, speaking out loud the thing that Ben had been thinking since early this morning, when he'd come into the Baxter Building to find Reed gone and Max hurriedly setting up the demonstration.

"Ninety-two-point-six-percent chance," Max agreed. "Give or take a half point."

"He's supposed to wait for us," Yates said. "We're a team, aren't we?"

"Yeah, we're a team," Ben said. "Come on. Let's go see if we can get him out."

The three of them, moving as one for the first time all day, started for the lab door.

5

THE FANTASTIC FOUR—THE NAME THE PRESS had given them after the accident, the name Yates, ever mindful of publicity, had suggested they adopt—owned the top four floors of the Baxter Building, in the heart of midtown Manhattan. They referred to those floors, bottom to top, as A, B, C, D. A was android fabrication, power plant, stores, redundant computer core. B was the only floor visitors were allowed on, the floor the three of them—Ben, Max, and Yates—were on now, which also contained the group's command center and living quarters for each of them, as well as a gym. The third floor—C—was labs—Reed's, Max's, and Yates's, though Ben couldn't for the life of him remember the last time Yates had been in it, there would have been cobwebs a foot thick if it wasn't for the maintenance droids, who cleaned non-stop throughout the four floors—as well as the main computer room. The fourth floor was the staging area for training exercises and various airborne vehicles. A stairway—metal rungs, surrounding the feeder conduit from the power plant on level A—ran through the center of the building connecting all four floors.

Ben leading the way, the three of them started up that staircase, heading from B to C, their footsteps clanging in the empty space. The sun shone down from above. The power plant hummed below.

At C, Ben stopped before a door that read:

AUTHORIZED ACCESS ONLY
DANGER

"I never get why the sign here," Ben said, punching in the entry code on the keypad next to the door. The lock clicked, and the door swung open.

"Just Reed, being careful," Yates said.

Ben nodded. Reed being careful; he hoped that was an omen. He hoped Reed had been careful this morning, too.

He stepped out into the access corridor. It ran in a circle around the core, offering access to each of the labs, which were arranged in spokes off the main hub.

"Where do we start?" Ben asked.

Yates pushed past him. "Come on. You know where he is."

He went left ten feet to another door. There was a sign on that one, too:

DANGER
ABSOLUTELY NO ACCESS
DANGER

The keypad next to it was flashing red.

"Ah, hell," Ben said, a sudden sinking feeling in his stomach. "He's in there, all right."

"He's been in there all morning?" Yates asked.

"At least," Max said. "I should have checked."

"You should have," Yates agreed.

"You're one to talk," Ben snapped. "At least Max was here. Where the heck were you?"

"Busy," Yates said. "Like I told you."

"Yeah, well . . ."

"Ben." Max put a hand on his arm. "Tony. Please. Let's go check observation. It's possible we can determine a course of action after assessing the situation."

Ben took a deep breath. "Yeah," he said finally. "Yeah, you're right. Let's check observation."

"A course of action?" Yates shook his head. "Like what?"

Ben ignored him, following Max left another twenty feet to a door marked "Lab 4." Max punched in the code, and they entered. Lab 4 was chem/genetics—a lot of gleaming steel counters and refrigerators, a lot of microscopes and scanning chambers—but they weren't interested in genetics right now, what they were interested in was visible through the glass off to their right, a pane some ten feet square, which looked out into the neighboring lab. Of course, it wasn't really glass, it was a special composite Reed had developed, one that was composed of both matter and antimatter, held in stasis by a continuously applied power field, thus allowing the glass literally to exist in two dimensions at once, the chem lab here . . .

And the Negative Zone beyond.

The three men looked through that glass, at what lay beyond, and froze as one in their tracks.

"What happened?" Ben asked. "Where is it?"

Max shook his head wordlessly.

"Must be something wrong with the portal," Yates said. "That's it. That has to be it."

"There's nothing wrong with the portal."

The voice came from behind them, so sudden and surprising that Ben almost jumped a mile. Reed's voice.

He smiled. "Stretch," he said, and turned.

Reed stood there, smiling, too, none the worse for wear.

"You sonuva . . . you had me worried there, you know, we don't hear from you all morning, and the portal light is on, and . . ."

Ben rushed forward to embrace his friend, and his arms went right through him.

Hologram.

"I'm in medical," Reed said. "Sorry."

"You're all right, though?" Max asked.

"I'm fine."

"You're fine, but what happened there?" Yates asked, pointing toward the glass and the Negative Zone, or, rather, where the Negative Zone should have been, because in place of the entire universe normally visible through the portal, the reds and oranges of antimatter suns, the blues and greens of antimatter worlds, the silver and gold of antimatter spaceships, there was now only blackness, an empty, lifeless void.

The Reed hologram—of course, it was a hologram, Ben didn't know why he hadn't seen that right away, it was the same hologram Reed always used for visitors, himself as he'd looked right after the space flight, not as he looked now—stood stock-still a moment before responding.

"At oh-three-forty-five this morning, the lab registered massive energy fluctuations within the portal. I'd prompted the system to wake me if anything like that happened; I got up here in time to see that the entire universe was literally falling apart."

"Universes don't fall apart," Max said.

"Colloquialism," Reed said. "I should have said that the fundamental particles of matter within the N-Zone were destabilizing."

"Was there a locatable center to the phenomenon?" Max asked.

"Initially. But . . ."

"It spread."

"Precisely."

"Unbelievable." Max shook his head. "You're talking actual decoherence of nuclear structure?"

"I am."

"You guys want to switch back to English for a second?" Ben put in. "Tell me what happened?"

"He went in." Max shook his head. "Reed. You should have called."

"You were home," Reed said. "You were with Rose. I was here."

Max opened his mouth to protest.

"Besides," Reed said, going on quickly. "I had every intention of calling. But things happened so fast. I got up here, and the Tyrannans were on the commlink. They were frantic."

"So you went in," Ben said.

"That's right. But"—Reed, the hologram, shook his head—"I didn't get far. Just past the second gateway"—there were four, Ben knew, physical barriers to protect their universe from the antimatter one—"there was an explosion. No, check that. *Explosion* isn't the right word. It was bigger than that. It was . . ." He shook his head again. "I passed out. The autopilot brought me back through the gateway, but when I tried to reestablish contact with the Tyrannans . . ."

"They were gone," Yates said.

"Not just the Tyrannans. They were all gone. Tennyson, Maximus, the Ketharans—everyone I tried to contact. The whole universe."

Ben looked over at the glass and the void beyond.

"I don't get it. How does a universe just . . . go?"

"I don't know," Reed said. "But I'm going to find out, once I get out of here."

Ben frowned. "Huh?"

"Decontamination," Reed said. "Max, you can start pulling the data together, if you would. We'll need to—"

"Whoa, whoa," Ben interrupted. "Decontamination? I thought you were fine."

"I am fine. Just a little radiation exposure, from the explosion," Reed said. "Nothing major."

Ben and Max exchanged a look.

Nothing major. That was what Reed said after Elizabeth, too.

"You're in medical?" Max said. "I want to take a look."

"No," Reed said quickly.

"Reed . . ."

"Max, please." Reed cleared his throat. "I just . . . I would prefer to be by myself for a while."

"You're always by yourself," Ben blurted out. "Reed . . ."

"It's all right." Max was looking at the palm screen. He held his hand up so Ben could see, too.

PATIENT STATUS RICHARDS, it read.

ROENTGEN EXPOSURE: MINIMAL.

CONDITION: STABLE.

EXPECTED DISCHARGE HOUR: 11:45 A.M.

That was about an hour from now.

Ben sighed. "All right. Be by yourself for a while."

"Thank you," Reed said.

"Till lunch."

"I would prefer . . ."

"Lunch," Ben said. "The four of us, together. Yes?"

Max nodded. Yates rolled his eyes.

"Good," Ben said. "We'll order from downstairs."

"Not Theo's," Yates said. "Anywhere but Theo's."

"May I point out we have more important things to discuss than lunch," Max said. "Specifically, what happened this morning, at the demonstration. Reed, there was a . . ."

"I saw," he said.

"You saw?" Ben frowned. "Then why didn't you . . ."

"I was trying to reestablish communication with the Tyrannans. By the time I had determined that would not be possible, Diehl had already escaped. Which also should not have been possible—not after the precautions Stephen and I took."

"Well, it happened," Yates said. "So maybe we need to strengthen whatever sorts of barriers you and Strange put up."

"That's a good idea," Reed said. "Do you think you could handle that?"

"Strange and I didn't exactly see eye-to-eye when he was here," Yates said. "Better if you do it."

"I'd prefer to focus on the Negative Zone investigation," Reed said.

"Reed," Yates said. "Believe me. I'll just irritate him. He'll think I'm criticizing what he did already."

"Not if you tell him what happened."

"I don't think so," Yates said. "Better if you do it."

Here we go again, Ben thought.

Yates couldn't—wouldn't—take direction from Reed. From anyone. Understandable, Ben supposed. Before the accident, Yates had run a multimillion-dollar corporation. He was always the man in charge—the smartest, the strongest-willed, the one everybody looked to for direction.

Not in the FF.

In the FF, on a good day, he was second man on the totem pole, and, more often than not, third behind Max.

The FF was Reed's show, no matter how many more headlines Yates grabbed, everybody knew that. Yates just couldn't handle that, and so—

"I'll call him," Ben said. "What the heck."

"Good," Reed said.

"Ross will want to reschedule the demonstration," Max said. "I'm sure he'll be calling."

"I think we ought to table that for the moment," Reed said. "Until we handle the security issues. And the Negative Zone investigation."

"He won't be happy," Max said.

"He's never happy," Ben said.

"You know what just occurred to me," Yates said. "Rikers. Diehl came from Building Twelve, right?"

"Right," Ben said.

"I've made some contacts there over the last few days," Yates said. "There may be some information there to uncover. Regarding the increase in his powers."

"Okay," Reed said.

"So that's what I'm going to do," Yates declared. "Check that out."

"If you're waiting for my permission," Reed began.

"I'm not," Yates said. "I just wanted to tell you where I was going."

Without another word, he turned and headed for the exit.

"I guess this means lunch is out, huh?" Ben called after him.

Yates went through the door without responding.

"Looks like it's just the three of us," Ben said.

"Right," Max said. "The three of us."

But Reed didn't show for lunch, either.

He got out of medical, went into the Negative Zone chamber again—by himself—and wouldn't come out.

Max worked in the computer core on C and barely looked up when Ben dropped by at one to see if he was hungry. He wasn't, so Ben ordered up a burger for himself and returned to the command center, where he spent the day trying to locate Strange.

Right before dinner, Sitwell called.

"I'll bet Ross is all over you, huh?" Ben said. "Listen—just tell him that because of security issues, the quantum computer demonstration is . . ."

"That's not why I'm calling," Sitwell said. "I heard you were looking for Doctor Strange."

"You heard right."

"He's behind the Curtain."

"Europe, you mean?"

"Eastern Europe, yes."

"What's he doing there?"

"If I told you," Sitwell said slowly, "I'd have to kill you."

"Hardy-har-har," Ben said. He could guess for himself, anyway.

The Curtain was the demarcation line—the border between the free states and Imperial Russia, which, since Doom had taken over, was even more Imperial than it had been under the tsars.

"When's he coming back?" Ben asked.

Sitwell actually giggled. "If I told you, I'd have to . . ."

"Right, right," Ben said. "I got it. Thanks for the info."

He hung up, and then called up to Reed, who didn't answer. Max didn't answer, either.

They were probably both in the Negative Zone

chamber now, Ben thought. Maybe they'd even gone out past the portal again, to see what they could see.

Some team, he thought.

He called home. Alicia answered on the first ring.

"Hey," he said.

"Hey, yourself."

Ben smiled. "I'm on my way."

"I'm right here," she said, and hung up.

6

EIGHT WEEKS AFTER THE FACT, ARMY PLANES were still flying circles around Elizabeth, to enforce the quarantine—nobody in, nobody out. Ben saw them as he took the speedboat across the river, from the pier on Fifty-first Street over to Hoboken. He docked and drove home.

Alicia was as good as her word. She was waiting for him. So were the kids. They came running down the stairs as he walked in the front door. Benjy and Tatianna. They jumped into his arms and squeezed him tight. He squeezed back, just a tiny bit.

And all at once, he had a feeling of vertigo, queasiness, nausea, a sense of something wrong in the world like he'd never had before in his life.

He sat right down in the middle of the hallway, still holding the kids in his arms, and tried to compose himself.

They were laughing. They thought it was a game.

Alicia knew better.

"Ben?" She leaned over, a look of concern, verging on panic, on her face. "Ben, honey, what is it? What's wrong?"

Everything, he wanted to say. *Everything is wrong.* The words were on his lips, but he couldn't get them out.

And then all he could do was make a joke of it.

"These kids," he said. "They weigh a ton."

He threw Benjy high up in the air with one hand and caught him. The boy shrieked with laughter. Then he did the same to Tatianna.

"Again!" she yelled. "Again!"

"After dinner." Ben got to his feet. Alicia was still staring at him. He looked away from her, and at the kids. "So how was school?"

"I made a rock," Benjy said.

"You made a rock." Ben frowned.

"No, no, no," Alicia said. "You painted a rock."

"Right," Benjy said. "I painted a rock. Can we have pizza for dinner?"

"I threw a rock," Tatianna said. "It hit Mr. Wilkins. He was very angry."

"We've already discussed this at length," Alicia said. "You won't do that again, will you, Tatianna?"

"No, ma'am."

"Good. Now, why don't you kids go wash your hands, and we'll eat."

"Is it pizza?" Benjy asked. "'Cause I want pizza."

"You always want pizza," Tatianna said. "You're gonna turn into a pizza."

"You're going to turn into a girl."

"I am not."

"Are too."

They went off toward the bathroom, bickering on the way.

Ben made to follow; Alicia stepped in his path.

"Ben?"

He shook his head. "It's nothing. I'm all right."

"Don't give me that. Tell me the truth. They're evacuating us, too, aren't they?"

"Evacuating?" he asked, suddenly realizing the source of her concern—the Elizabeth quarantine. The army had already cleared a ring three miles wide around the city, or where the city used to be, anyway, and rumors were going around—Ben heard some of them for himself the other morning, when the speedboat broke down and he'd crossed the river in a hired water taxi, along with two dozen neighbors—that they were going to expand that ring, maybe right up to the Hudson. The people on the boat over had been frantic—Ben saw the same worry in his wife's eyes now.

"No, they're not evacuating us," he said. "Believe me. There was an army general at the Baxter Building today—the situation is stable."

"Well . . ." She frowned. "Okay, then. But if it's not an evacuation, what's the matter, honey? You looked so worried there for a minute."

He hesitated a second, then lied.

"I don't know what it was. Just—just a crazy day today, I guess," he said, and went on to tell her about it. Just a few seconds into the story about Jembay Diehl, though, he realized why he was lying.

He was scared to death—of what, exactly, he wasn't sure, but it had something to do with Alicia and Benjy and Tatianna. His family. His world.

He thought about the Tyrannans then, and the Negative Zone. A whole universe—there one minute and gone the next.

"Ben?"

He forced himself to smile. "Yeah?"

"You sure you're all right?"

"No. I'm starving. Is it pizza?"

Alicia smiled, too, and punched him on the arm. "Go wash up. You'll see."

It wasn't pizza, it was lasagna, but that was all right. Benjy ate two helpings, so did Tatianna, and Ben ate three—pans of it, that is.

They watched *Animal Planet* for half an hour and then went upstairs. Ben read the kids a story and put them to bed, while Alicia went down to her studio in the basement to paint.

He stopped off at the fridge for a beer, before heading down to join her.

One beer turned into two. He was still—after the dinner, after the time with the kids—on edge. Worried. He couldn't figure out why.

It wasn't security, that was for sure. There were two O'Hoolihans on neighborhood patrol 24/7, a Roberta that was doing household work in the spare room right now, another that followed the kids to school, and another that nobody but Ben knew about up in the attic, a specially programmed Roberta that had a lot of what Max had called "accoutrements" when he'd handed her over to Ben. Sharp, explosive accoutrements. So his family was safe, even when he wasn't here. That normally gave Ben peace of mind. Not tonight.

He was frowning as he came down the stairs.

The basement of their brownstone was split in half—her studio, his workroom. Hers was at the bottom of the stairs, his through a door in the wall they'd built bisecting the basement space.

Alicia was so focused on her work she didn't even hear him come down the stairs, and that was saying something.

Ben studied his wife a second.

He'd met her at an art reception, about a year after the accident. One of Yates's "events," which all four of them—the Fantastic Four—had attended, back when they were all living in the Baxter Building, all friends, all trying to be good teammates. Partners. It had been some sort of benefit, Ben couldn't even remember for what now, Yates had gotten up to talk, gone on and on and on, and Ben finally had excused himself.

He was on his way out the door, and a woman was on her way in. They'd run smack into each other. Less gracious in those days—well, really, back then he'd been a jerk, and he might have had one drink too many that night—Ben had bumped right into her.

"Hey," he said. "Why don't you watch where you're . . ."

At which point his voice trailed off, and he'd found himself blushing brighter than he would have thought humanly possible, because the woman he'd just bumped into was, in fact, blind. Blind, and blindingly beautiful.

He wasn't so much of a jerk that he didn't try to apologize, but somehow the words didn't come out exactly the way he wanted them to. The apology turned into an argument, which turned into a long discussion about the "privileges" the woman—whose name turned out to be Alicia Masters—thought Ben and the other members of the FF were unrightfully assuming were theirs.

The argument had turned into a conversation, which was new for Ben, as ever since the accident, he hadn't had women do much other than fawn over him. A week after Yates's event, he'd called Alicia for a date. Coffee, the Starbucks on Madison and Thirty-second. More arguments, more conversation, and at last, a little information about her: Alicia was a sculptor, it turned out. She'd been blinded in an accident involving her stepfather, the details of which were rather hazy to Ben.

On their second date, he took her to dinner at the Rainbow Room.

On their third, he flew her to Paris.

On their fourth, he proposed.

A month after they got back from their honeymoon, Max walked into the gym on B level and plopped a folder on Ben's chest.

"What's this?" Ben asked, opening it up.

"Corneal replacement," Max said. "It occurred to me that the operating protocol they've developed over at Roosevelt for burn victims could be used for other purposes. Such as this."

Ben blinked.

Alicia, when he told her, cried.

She had the operation a week later, and just like that—

"I see you there, you know," she said suddenly, without turning around. "Lurking. What's on your mind?"

"I'm not lurking," Ben said.

"You're definitely lurking. With ulterior motives, I have no doubt."

"Ulterior motives? Me?" He walked up behind

Alicia and bent down. He kissed the nape of her neck. "I'm a straightforward kind of guy."

"Mmmm." She smiled without turning. "Yeah. That's you, all right. Mr. Straightforward."

He kissed her again.

She put down the brush.

"You think the kids are asleep yet?" she asked.

He smiled.

"Who cares?"

She smiled back.

The doorbell rang.

Ben growled.

Alicia frowned. "Who could that be at this hour?"

He had no idea. It was Tuesday, so it couldn't be Max, Max was Thursdays. It couldn't be Reed, because it was never Reed, and Yates wouldn't be caught dead in Jersey, he'd been gracious enough to say that to Alicia's face more than once, and if it was anyone from the neighborhood, they'd know to call first, and if it was anyone looking for trouble, well, they wouldn't really bother ringing the bell, would they?

Ben walked to the wall and activated the monitor.

It was Max.

He pressed the intercom.

"Wrong day, genius," Ben said.

"Yes. I realize that, I . . . I'm sorry to disturb you, Ben. I wonder if I could have a moment."

Ben was about to say no when he took a closer look at the monitor.

Something was wrong. He could tell from the way Max was standing.

Alicia leaned over his shoulder and spoke.

"Hi, Max," she said. "Come on in. Have some tea."

He smiled. "That would be lovely."

"Yes," Ben growled. "Lovely."

It came out harsher than he intended. Max's face fell.

"If now is inconvenient . . ."

"Now is fine," Alicia said. "Just ignore my husband and his feeble attempts at humor."

She buzzed him in, then turned back to Ben.

"You could have been a little more gracious."

"Sorry. I just . . ." He lost the words somewhere between his brain and his tongue.

I wanted you, he'd meant to say. *To myself. Now, because I'm afraid that if . . .*

He didn't know what he was afraid of.

Alicia went up on tiptoe and kissed his cheek.

"I know," she said, reading his mind, as always. "Don't worry. The night is young."

She headed up the stairs.

He managed a smile, and followed.

The three of them went into the kitchen. They all had tea. They made small talk—Max asked after the kids, and Alicia responded with a chapter-and-verse summary of the latest, incredible, fantastic things Benjy and Tatianna had done, some of which Ben had heard before (the rock-throwing incident) and some of which he hadn't (Benjy reading the first chapter of *Charlotte's Web* aloud to his class). And then Alicia asked after Rose, and Max shifted uncomfortably in his seat.

"Rose," he said, and then shifted again. "She's fine. Oh, yes. Quite fine. Although worried. Her family's still in Prague, you know. And the news from Prague is not good. Not good at all."

Ben and Alicia exchanged a glance.

He was lying. Max was lying. Why?

"Yes," Alicia said. "I heard that. I heard Prague was—there was a crackdown. You ought to get them out, Max."

"Yes," he said. "I ought to. I've told that to Rose more than once. Her sister would come. It's her mother who won't leave. She says she outlasted the Nazis, she outlasted the Communists, she'll outlast this, too. Maybe she will. Who knows. Maybe she will."

And then Max actually giggled. It was the oddest sound Ben had ever heard in his life. For one thing, Ben had known Max—what?—ten years or so, and the guy had actually laughed all of half a dozen times during that time. For another . . .

The giggle wasn't the sound made by somebody hopelessly amused.

It was more like the sound of desperation.

"Forgive me," Max said.

Ben leaned across the table. "You all right, buddy?"

His friend shook his head. "I'm not sure, to tell you the truth. I'm just not sure."

Max von Scharf. He was a couple of inches shy of six feet, maybe a hundred ninety pounds, long black hair, sometimes shading to brown, that he kept slicked back at all times. Thick, Eastern European features. Trace of an English accent, because the von Scharf family that had brought him up—Max was adopted—had lived mainly in London while Max was a kid. While he and Rose were kids, upper-upper-middle-class kids, raised in the midst of all the culture Europe had to offer before the world on the other side of the Atlantic got dark and life got hard.

Which was one way of saying that Max was always, always, immaculately turned out. His hair immaculately coiffed.

Except at that instant, Max von Scharf looked like hell.

"What is it, Max?" Alicia asked.

He cleared his throat.

"Well," he said finally. "The thing of it is, Rose and I have had a fight."

Is that all? Goes with the territory, Ben was about to say, the territory meaning marriage, but bit back the words when he realized how flippant they would sound and saw how deadly serious Max looked.

"Every couple has fights," Alicia said gently, putting Ben's sentiments into better words. "Whatever was said . . . you just—you work it out. You talk it out."

"Yes, well . . ." Max sighed heavily. "That's just the thing. Nothing was said."

Ben frowned.

"You had a fight, and nothing was said?"

Max nodded. "Yes."

"I don't get it."

"It was my fault," Max said. "All my fault."

He looked absolutely miserable. He stared down at the table.

Ben looked at Alicia; she widened her eyes, nodded at Max.

Ben got the message: *Say something.* But he didn't know what to say.

Alicia rolled her eyes.

"Oh," she said suddenly. "That boy."

Ben blinked. "Huh?"

"Benjy," she said, and pushed her chair back from the table. "He's still playing on the gamecue—can't you hear him? Excuse me a minute, Max, I'll be right back," she said, and headed for the stairs, pausing in the entryway long enough to shoot a significant glance in Max's direction before disappearing.

There was another minute of silence.

"Gamecue," Max said. "That's one of those electronic gadgets, isn't it? I thought you weren't going to get Benjy one of those."

"We didn't."

Max looked up; both men smiled.

Ben got to his feet.

"Where are you going?" Max asked.

He dumped his tea in the sink.

"I had a beer around here somewhere," he said. "I'm gonna find it. You want one?"

"You know I don't drink."

"I know you don't usually drink. You want a beer?"

Max hesitated a second.

"Do you have cognac?"

"Cognac? I don't know. I can check."

Ben went to the liquor cabinet. There were a whole bunch of funny-shaped bottles in the back; he pulled a few out and found one, covered with dust, that turned out to be cognac indeed. Then he pulled out a glass they'd gotten as a wedding present and never used, poured what he judged to be a good amount of the cognac into it, and brought it back to the kitchen.

"A proper snifter," Max said. "I'm impressed."

"Ben Grimm—the height of Jersey sophistication," he said, and raised his bottle. "Cheers."

"Cheers," Max said. Glass clinked together, and they drank.

"So," Ben said, setting his beer down on the table. "This no-word fight . . ."

Max swirled the cognac in his glass. He took another sip—and another long moment before answering.

"I came home tonight," Max said, "and I took Rose in my arms, and I had—all at once—the strangest feeling."

Bottle halfway to his lips, Ben froze.

A chill crept up his spine.

"I felt as if I didn't belong with her. I . . ."

No, Ben thought, and put the bottle back down on the table. *No, no, no.* He did not want to hear this. What he had felt walking into the house before dinner, what Max was describing . . .

His friend was still talking.

". . . she saved me. When I was a boy . . . what I would have become without her . . ." Max took another long, slow sip of the cognac and shook his head. "Absolutely crazy, isn't it?"

"Yeah," Ben managed.

"Yeah is right. Well. I feel better for having told you, at least. For saying it out loud like that. It does sounds ridiculous. So . . . thank you for listening, Ben."

"Hey. No problem," he said, feeling suddenly nauseated himself. "What are friends for?"

"That's right," Max said. "What are friends for?"

He drained the last of his cognac in a single swallow, set the glass down on the table, and smiled up at Ben.

"So. I know it's a few days early, but . . . how about a game?"

They went down to Ben's workroom, which was a misnomer, inasmuch as anything related to work—the handyman sort, the sort requiring the tools, machines, and supplies that the room had originally been designed to accommodate—was still in boxes, or stacked in corners, or hidden from sight. There were sawhorses on the perimeter of the room, planks on the sawhorses, and game boards on the planks. Checker boards, specifically, twenty-four of them, each with a game in progress.

The two of them had been playing since the day before the space flight, before the accident that changed everything. Ten years ago Ben and Max had been in the lounge; Reed and Yates had been off checking the landing module for when they got to Mars. Max, who had spent twenty of the last twenty-four hours doing a line-by-line review of the ship's computer code, was on a mandated break, and Ben was watching an old episode of *Mission: Impossible.*

Max was pacing. He walked in front of the TV set in the lounge, momentarily blocking Ben's view.

"Hey," Ben said. "Do you mind?"

Max shook his head. "It's a waste of time."

Ben frowned. "Hey, look, pal—I don't tell you what to watch, so I'll thank you to . . ."

"Oh, no, I'm sorry," Max said, and stepped out of the way. "Not that, the show. This break. I should be on the ship, I should be going over the code. I was right in the middle of the environmental systems emergency subroutine calls, and then . . ."

"Scharf," Ben said. "Relax, okay? How many times have you been over those computers?"

"Two complete passes. I'm thirty-six point seven

percent of the way through a third, and unless I get back in there soon, I won't finish that pass before we launch."

Ben shook his head.

One obsessive supergenius per space flight next time, he told himself. Reed was hard enough to take, but at least he and Reed had history—four years at Empire State University. Plus this whole thing—the mission to Mars—was Reed's baby. Or at least it had been, till NASA had yanked funding, and Reed had to go in search of the money elsewhere. Enter Tony Yates, his pocketbook, and his own obsessive supergenius, Maximillian von Scharf, who stood in front of Ben now, shaking his head and muttering to himself.

Scharf didn't seem like a bad guy, though, Ben had to admit that. Unlike Yates, who'd rubbed him the wrong way from the word go. Yates thought his money made him head honcho on the flight; Scharf at least had the good sense—and the common courtesy—to recognize that Reed had been at this for three years, and so was maybe entitled to at least a little deference from time to time.

"You could do some of it for me," Scharf said. "Go on the ship, I'll tell you which monitor to—"

"Not likely," Ben said.

On the screen, Peter Graves was just peeling off his face and Lynda Day George was smoothing down her skirt. Good-looking woman, Lynda Day George.

The credits came up. He switched the TV off.

Scharf was still pacing.

"Relax," Ben said again.

"I'm reviewing the code in my mind," Scharf said. "So that when I get back on the ship, I'll have a head start on it."

"Reviewing the code in your mind?"

"The ideal code. The code as it should be. I'm pinpointing areas of possible confusion." Scharf smiled apologetically. "I have a photographic memory."

"You have an obsessive-compulsive disorder." Ben's gaze went around the room and landed on the game closet. Yates had set it up for their families—really for his family, as he was the only one married. Wife named Amara, who seemed nice enough but didn't smile a lot, and three kids, whose names Ben had immediately forgotten. "Let's see if we can find you something else to think about."

He opened the closet, and pulled out a chess set. "What do you think?"

Scharf raised an eyebrow.

"You. Want to play me in chess?"

"Yeah." Ben shrugged. "I played a little in college."

Inwardly, he smiled. He'd played more than a little in college; he'd been on the team. Third-ranked, behind Reed and Todd Olshavsky, and he'd beaten Olshavsky senior year three out of five matches.

Ben took white. Scharf took black. Ben made one move, Scharf made another. Ben made a second, so did Scharf, and then the man cleared his throat and said, "Checkmate."

Ben looked at the board. None of Scharf's pieces was anywhere near his king.

"Huh?" he said.

"Checkmate," Scharf said again. "In four moves."

Ben looked again. He still didn't see it.

Scharf showed him.

"Okay." So he was rusty. Ben set the pieces up again.

Ten moves.

They played again.

Eight moves.

"I could give you a handicap," Scharf said. "Play without my queen, for instance."

"No," Ben said, keeping his lips clenched tight so the frustration he felt inside wouldn't boil out. "How about a different game?"

There were cards in the closet, too. Ben thought briefly about poker, but decided that wouldn't be to his advantage, considering his opponent's photographic memory. Gin rummy, same thing. Monopoly, Candyland, an old Captain America game . . .

And a little cardboard box. Ben opened it and found a set of checkers inside.

"Here's something," he said, and spilled the checkers out onto the board.

"What are those?"

"Checkers," Ben said, putting the chess pieces into the cardboard box. "You never played checkers?"

Max shook his head.

"Okay," Ben said. "Then we'll learn."

He set the men on the board.

"Now, a lot of people think it's a kid's game. But there's strategy to checkers, too."

He explained the rules.

Scharf frowned. "Please don't be offended, but—it does seem rather simplistic."

"Let's play a game," Ben said. "And I'll show you."

He showed him.

The openings, the middle play, the end game. The positions, the strategy, and the traps; the Kelso, the Bristol-Cross, the Edinburgh-Lassie. Ben had learned them when he was a kid, first from his Aunt Penny and then from every book he could lay his hands on. In college, his interest had switched over to chess, but even though he hadn't played in years, all the knowledge, all the old terminology, had come rushing back to him the second he'd sat behind the board and moved his first man.

He won the first three games.

Then Max got it.

He won thirty-six out of the next thirty-seven before Colonel Talbot poked his head in and told them they were late for dinner.

They brought the game on board the ship but never had a chance to take it out. The accident.

It was a month later—a Thursday night, after they were back, after the accident that had changed everything—before they finally got a chance to play again.

They'd been playing every Thursday night since.

Max walked to the center of the workroom and closed his eyes.

"Ready."

Ben crossed to a board with a red *8* taped to the front of it.

"Game eight," he said.

"Eight." Max nodded. "All right."

They each had half a dozen men remaining on the board, all kings. Ben was red, Max black.

"Fifteen-eighteen," Ben said, and moved his piece, fifteen being the space where his man had come from, eighteen where he was going. In checkers, the dark spaces—the only ones the men could move on—were also the only ones that were numbered. One to twenty-four, moving from left to right, starting at the single dark square in the upper left of the board.

"Your move."

Max frowned. He had ten seconds to incorporate Ben's move into the mental picture of this game in his head, and then to make his own. One of the ways that, over the years, they'd evened the odds in the game, so that Ben was able—every once in a great, great while—to take a game.

Max made a *tsk*-ing noise. "Ah. You're trying to sucker me in, aren't you?" He shook his head. "Seven-nine."

Max moved.

Ben frowned

"You need to jump," Max said, then gave him the move. "Then I double-jump, thirteen-sixteen. Then—"

Ben growled. "Yeah, I see it," he said, and swept all the men off the board and into a waiting box with a lot more force than was necessary.

Max opened his eyes.

"Ben? Is everything all right?"

He almost said it then. *The same thing you felt with Rose, I felt with Alicia. With the kids. Something is wrong, Max. Something is very wrong.*

Instead, he looked away, and lied.

"I'm fine," he said. "It's Reed I'm worried about. That whole thing with the Negative Zone this morning . . ."

"I know," Max said. "He's withdrawing again, Ben. He hasn't left the building since . . . since I don't know when."

"I do," Ben said. "Since Elizabeth. We gotta get him to come out of that lab once in a while."

"Perhaps a vacation?" Max suggested.

"Perhaps a girlfriend."

"One might get him the other."

"Are you suggesting we send Reed to Club Med?"

Both men laughed.

Ben set game eight up again. He showed it to Max—let him visualize the physical idiosyncrasies of the pieces and the board, which Max said helped him keep each game distinct in his mind. Why they played games in the real world, rather than on a computer.

They went around the room, making three moves to each board. Two games played out to endings; Ben lost both badly. He made stupid moves, amateur moves. Max asked again if there was anything wrong. Again, Ben lied.

He felt that if he told the truth, it would somehow make it real.

They said good night. Ben shut the door on his friend and turned for the stairs.

The light on the answering machine was blinking. They had a message.

He played it back.

"Ben Grimm. You blockhead. It's Johnny Storm. Pick up the phone." There was a pause. "Come on, I know you're there, pick up the phone." Another pause. "All right. Never mind. Listen, I'm in town. Here's the number where I'm staying. I want you to call me . . ."

Ben hit the pause button. Johnny Storm. How long had it been? Ten years? Since right after the accident, that was the last time he'd spoken to Johnny. Storm had been one of Ben's students at flight school. Good pilot. Smart-ass, though. Always with the jokes. Still, there was something about the kid that Ben liked. He'd take Storm over any of the stamped-out-of-a-mold, yessir, nosir types NASA had sent him any day. Johnny had spirit.

And then there was his sister.

And thinking about Johnny Storm's sister, Ben

thought about Reed again, and what had happened right after the accident, and realized it wasn't just Elizabeth that had changed everything for his friend.

He decided that it wouldn't be such a good idea to return Johnny's call. Another time, maybe. A less tense time.

He erased the message and went upstairs to bed, where he had a fitful, dream-filled night's sleep.

7

THE NEXT MORNING, THOUGH, THE BIRDS WERE singing, the sun was shining, and all was right with the world.

Ben woke up early and made breakfast for the family. Belgian waffles. He drenched them with strawberries and syrup and whipped cream. Benjy and Tatianna bounced up and down in their chairs, waiting for their plates.

"All that sugar? On a school morning?" Alicia frowned. "Ben, I'm not sure . . ."

He smothered her mouth—and her objections—with a kiss.

"I made one for you, too," he said, and marched her over to the table.

The three of them ate and went off, the kids to school, the Roberta trailing dutifully behind, Alicia to her yoga class.

Ben cleaned up, worked out himself, and took the speedboat into the city.

He got to the Baxter Building, stopping at Theo's for breakfast and a quick chat with Olga, before heading up to the command center to start looking for Strange again.

The second he logged on, the Reed hologram appeared in front of him.

"Not necessary, Ben," it said. "I found him last night."

"You found him. Doctor Strange we're talking about?"

"Yes. He's in Leningrad. We spoke at some length, regarding yesterday's intrusion."

"How did you find him?" Ben asked. "I spent all day . . ."

"S.H.I.E.L.D."

"You mean, Sitwell told you where he was?"

"No." The hologram shook its head. "I hacked into their network. Strange knows him, Ben."

"Huh?"

"Jembay Diehl. Strange knows him. Or knew him twenty years ago, at least. Said there was no way he should have been able to get through our defenses. He's simply not powerful enough."

"That's not news. We knew that yesterday. The guy

got stronger, that's all. Did some mystic training, or whatever. Like you said—it's been twenty years."

"No." The hologram shook its head. "Stephen was quite firm on that point. There are only a handful of sorcerers powerful enough to get through the shields he set up for us, and he can name them all."

"Yeah," Ben said. "I could name them, too, probably, on one finger of one hand. Four-letter word, rhymes with *room,* wears a green cloak—"

"It's simply not possible," Reed continued, ignoring the interruption, "for someone to acquire that kind of power without him knowing about it."

"So how did Diehl do it?"

"Stephen had a few thoughts on that subject as well. He suggested," the Reed hologram said, starting to pace, "that we examine surveillance footage of the incident."

Ben stood just as the Reed hologram turned, and strode right through him.

"Hey. You mind if we have this conversation in person? It's a little disconcerting being able to walk through the person you're talking to."

The hologram wavered a second.

"That isn't necessary. I have visual through the computer link."

"Tell me you're not in the Negative Zone again."

"Ben." The hologram managed to look exasperated. "There is no Negative Zone anymore. Remember?"

"Right. So where are you?"

The hologram wavered again.

"Medical."

"Medical? Why? What's the matter?"

"Nothing serious. Antiradiation treatment. Just getting a second dose, after yesterday."

Ben frowned. Max had looked at the readout last night and said it was nothing serious, too, but . . .

"I'm coming up," Ben said, heading for the core and the stairs up to C level.

"I'm in isolation," Reed called after him.

"So?"

"So you can't get in."

Ben spun around.

"Reed. Stop with the games, already. If you're hurt, let me help. Let somebody help."

"I'm fine."

"Then why won't you let me see you?"

There was a pause.

"The radiation treatment has some side effects. Aesthetically unpleasing. I'd rather be alone, until they wear off."

"Reed . . ."

"Ben. Please."

Dammit, Ben thought. This was just what happened after the accident, Reed hiding himself away, refusing to see anybody.

"I'm coming up."

"You won't get in."

"I'll get in," Ben said. He'd get Max to help him; it

was Max's system. Even Reed couldn't lock Max out.

He got to C and went to the computer core.

Max wasn't there.

"Max isn't here." Reed's voice came from behind him; Ben turned and saw the hologram again.

"I can see that. Where is he?"

"I don't know."

"He's probably home," Ben said. Sleeping in. After the cognac . . .

"He's not."

"What?"

"Rose called here this morning, looking for him. Said they had a fight last night, and he never came back."

Ben sat down.

The Thinker, out on a drunk. Wait till the *Daily Bugle* got hold of that.

"We gotta find him," Ben said.

"I've initiated a search," Reed said. "A very intensive search."

"I'll call Danny," Ben said, meaning his brother, who had all sorts of contacts at the police department. He reached for the phone and frowned. If he called Danny, Max being missing was official. Official wasn't good. Official meant on-the-record, meant people talking, meant publicity.

"Ben," the hologram said. "Believe me. I've got it covered. A lot of people are looking for him. You know Max. He probably said something cross to Rose and is regretting it."

"Yeah," Ben said. "I guess so."

He hoped so.

He banished the little chill of foreboding in the back of his mind and sighed.

"The most productive thing we can do," Reed said, "is work."

The monitor in front of Ben suddenly came to life.

"I'm starting playback at ten twenty-two A.M. yesterday. Five minutes before the attack," Reed said, and they watched—Ben in his chair, Reed via remote—as the events of yesterday morning unfolded all over again.

The most noteworthy thing about the whole recording, for Ben, was not the increase in Diehl's power, or his mood swings, or even his diatribe against Max. The most noteworthy thing occurred right as Diehl appeared out of nowhere, on the stage alongside the Q-Ray, looking—for a split second—utterly lost and confused.

The most noteworthy thing for Ben was the look on his own face as he stepped up onstage alongside the man.

It was the same look of utter confusion Diehl wore, and though it lasted only a split second—during which time, instead of hitting Diehl full-on, Ben pulled his punch—it was definitely there.

And that was noteworthy. No, not just noteworthy. Shocking.

Because Ben didn't remember feeling that way at all.

"Energy readings are off the scale here," Reed said, "at ten twenty-seven A.M., when Diehl appears. Then they drop off significantly for the duration of the fight, right up until here, his escape—" The images shifted, showing Diehl stretching, and then vanishing right out of the room. "—when they surge in intensity again. Though, of course, any measurement of eldritch energy by noneldritch instruments is going to give problematic results, or at least approximate ones."

Ben nodded, watching Diehl as he disappeared.

"Guy's nuts," Ben said. "Right? He wanted to destroy the Q-Ray to protect us. What sort of sense does that make?"

"Not a lot," Reed said.

On the monitor, Diehl screamed at Max.

"Because Max was going to use it to . . ." Ben shrugged. "What?"

"Give Ross his cipher."

"Or something like that." Ben sighed. "The guy's crazy, obviously. A loon."

"Of course."

There was something—a note of hesitation—in that "Of course" that made Ben turn around.

"What?"

"I did spend quite a bit of time reviewing the machine's schematics last night—its operating parameters."

"Busy night for you," Ben said. "Did you get any sleep?"

"An hour or two. I'm not certain."

"You think that could have anything to do with why you had to go back into medical?" Ben asked.

"The point being," the hologram continued, "I discovered that under certain conditions, the device could be used to project an exclusionary Hilbert space, which would—"

A distinctive electronic chirping sound from the corner of the room interrupted him.

Ben's head whipped around.

That was the sound of the FF's private commlink. Only four people had transceivers for it. Reed, Ben, Yates, and . . .

Max.

Ben breathed a sigh of relief.

He walked across the room and activated the device.

"Max," he said, as the screen came to life. "About time."

But it wasn't Max.

It was Yates.

The commlink showed his face, and an orange concrete wall, with a hole smashed through it, behind him. Ben heard screaming, and shouting, and gunfire.

"A little help here," Yates said, and then the screen went dark.

"That's Rikers," Reed said.

"Yeah. I recognize those walls, too. Let's go," Ben said, heading for the stairs again, and D level.

"I can't," Reed said.

Ben stopped in his tracks.

"Why not?"

"I can't leave the decontamination chamber," Reed said. "Not for another twenty-four hours."

"It's not just cosmetic, then," Ben said. "Is it?"

"No," Reed said. "It's not."

A world of different responses crossed Ben's mind, but he discarded them all in favor of a simple "You lied."

"Yes," Reed said. "I didn't want to worry you. I'm sorry, Ben."

"Yeah," he said, heading for the stairs. "So am I."

He was so pissed at Reed he forgot about the force shield above the island until the aerocar slammed into it, so hard Ben bit his tongue and tasted blood. He cursed out loud, looked down, and cursed again.

The entire island looked as if it was on fire.

Rikers was in the middle of the East River, between Queens and the Bronx. The only physical point of access was a small bridge leading to Queens, but Rikers didn't need all that much out of the mainland. The place was entirely self-sufficient, a little city of its own, with a power plant, a two-year supply of food and water, atmosphere-generating capability, police force (obviously), and sanitation crew. It was home to roughly fifteen thousand people, about fourteen thousand of whom were inmates, scattered among ten different correctional facilities on the island.

And then there was Building Twelve, where they kept the bad guys (and girls) who found concrete and metal not much of an obstacle at all. The supervillains.

"Building Twelve?" Ben had asked Flynn once. "Why is it twelve and not eleven?"

Flynn frowned. "There was a Building Eleven. Once."

"What happened to it?"

The man had simply shaken his head. "Trust me. You don't wanna know."

Ben brought the aerocar down as near to the Queens side of the bridge as he could get it; the access road was jammed full of police cars and emergency vehicles, and a bunch of blue uniforms standing around, looking anxiously across the water.

Heads turned as he approached. None of them looked happy. Some of them, in fact, looked downright mad. And unless he missed his guess . . .

Some of their anger, at least, was being directed at him.

Ben frowned. Something was off here.

One cop broke ranks and started forward.

"Freak!" he shouted at Ben, whose jaw dropped. He repeated the word and added a series of curses in front of it. "Why don't you go back to whatever circus you came from, 'cause the last thing we need here is the kind of help you—"

"Henderson!" Another cop—one with a gold shield—stepped out of the line, and put a hand on the first man's shoulder. "Back in line. That's an order."

The man shook off his superior's hand.

"Sir, we got half a dozen dead men because of this freak bastard's partner . . ."

"Henderson! Back in line." This time the cop with the gold shield—his nameplate said GRAD—put the hand down and spun the first man physically around so that the two were facing each other. "Now. Or I'll have your weapon, and I'll have you brought up on charges."

They glared at each other a moment. Half the cops on the line protecting the bridge glared, too. At Ben.

Half a dozen dead men because of this freak bastard's partner.

Yates, Ben thought. *What have you done now?*

Grad pushed the other man back in line and then approached Ben. He pulled him away from the bridge a hundred feet.

"As you can see," Grad said, "we have a situation."

"Yeah. Two of 'em at least. What's going on in there?" Ben nodded toward the island. "And what did Yates do?"

Grad shook his head. "I wasn't there, so I only got this secondhand."

"That's all right."

"What I was told, Yates showed up early this morning, went right to Building Twelve."

Ben nodded. Yates had said yesterday he was coming here to try to find out a little more about Jembay Diehl.

"He goes to Records, then he goes to see this guy Diablo. What happened next—I'm not entirely sure, a couple versions of the story are going around. The one that sounds right to me, the Torch and this Diablo go for a walk, only it's not really Diablo, it's just this kind of double he created—I guess this Diablo is a magician of some kind?"

"Yeah," Ben said. "He's a magician, all right."

Inwardly, he sighed. Of course, it was Diablo. His own karma coming back to haunt him—Ben was responsible for Diablo being a problem at all, Ben having been the one who'd set Diablo loose on the world in the first place. He and Alicia had been honeymooning over in Europe, they'd gone to this old castle and stumbled on a hidden passage, found this guy trapped in a containment field of some kind. Ben thought he was Merlin, out of the old King Arthur books, but he turned out to be some Spanish nobleman, something like that, who'd been trapped for centuries. "Set me free," the man had told Ben, "and I'll grant your fondest wish."

Ben, whose fondest wish was standing right beside him at that moment, thought instantly of Reed, and what the accident had done to him.

"Can you cure my friend?" he'd asked, describing the problem to Diablo, who assured him that such miracles were his stock-in-trade.

Of course, he'd been lying.

Once Ben set him free, he'd gone on a rampage. The FF caught him, and he did it again, and again, and again.

Last time, they'd taken him to Strange, who'd done something to the man, something that left Diablo a vacant-eyed, slack-jawed simpleton. At the time, Ben thought it a fitting punishment, but standing next to Grad now, watching the flames from Rikers lick at the sky, it suddenly seemed cruel to him. Wrong, in some fundamental way.

And again, for an instant, he had that same feeling of vertigo that had seized him yesterday, when his children jumped into his arms.

He shook his head to clear it. Grad was still talking.

". . . a hostage situation. We were gonna let him go, 'cause he had two men. Or his doubles had them. Your partner—how can I put this delicately—escalated the situation. So all of a sudden, we got two dead guards."

"Great," Ben said.

"Oh, that's not the best part. While this is going on, there's another one of these Diablos running around setting everyone loose."

"Everyone from Building Twelve is loose in there?" He frowned and reached for the commlink. *Avengers,* he thought. *X-Men. Spider-Man, even, if we can get hold of him, because if everyone from Building Twelve is out, that's a lot more than the FF at full strength, never mind half, can handle.*

"No, no," Grad said. "Not everyone from Building Twelve. Just the psych ward. The loonies. Where Diablo was. So really, what we got in there is kind of a . . ."

"Madhouse," Ben finished for him. "Okay. Someone have an overall strategic picture? Where Diablo is, where your men are?"

Grad shook his head. "No. We got no contact with the island whatsoever."

"Let me see what I have," Ben said, and pressed the commlink on his wrist. Just static. So the Torch was still either busy fighting, or his commlink was damaged, or . . .

There was a sudden rumble like thunder, deep beneath the ground. An explosion from across the river.

"One of the fuel storage tanks," Grad said. "Sounds like to me."

"All right," Ben said. "I'm going in. You guys monitor emergency channels—I'll talk to you on them."

He started toward the bridge.

"Hold on," Grad said. "You better let me walk with you. Just in case."

Not necessary, Ben was about to say, when he looked up and saw the row of angry-looking cops, still staring at him.

"Okay," he told Grad. "I guess that's not such a bad idea."

Grad took him to the bridge; Ben crossed by himself, through a gateway in the force shield and onto Rikers Island proper. There was smoke everywhere, thick as molasses; acrid and foul-smelling. The guard at the end of the bridge had given him a mask, but the mask made it hard for him to breathe at all, so after wearing it for less than twenty seconds, Ben chucked it to the ground. He was on the main north-south service road; it ran from the bridge to the other side of the island, where Building Twelve was, as far from the mainland and the rest of the detention facilities as they could put it.

He took a step forward, and his commlink crackled.

"Ben."

He'd expected Yates, but it was Reed.

"Go," he said.

"I just repositioned one of our satellites geosynchronous to you and tied in to Rikers communications network. So any information you need . . ."

"Their network's down."

"I forced a link through," Reed said. "Any information you need, say the word."

"Good," Ben said, and coughed.

"You have a mask on, don't you?"

"Relax. It's just a little smoke."

"I have visual. It looks like a lot of smoke."

"Can we argue about something else, please?"

"I have your position," Reed said. "You want Building Twelve, which is due north of you, about a quartermile. The main road you're on gets there, but a quicker way there is—"

"Reed," Ben interrupted.

"Yes?"

"Any information I need, you said."

"Right."

"I haven't asked for any information yet."

"Ah." There was silence over the link for a second. "Leave you alone, in other words."

"No, just let me concentrate. I gotta stay alert. Focused." He looked up through the smoke and frowned, and coughed again. "Can't see much more than a hundred feet in front of me."

"Roger that," Reed said. "I'm here if you need me."

"I'm sure I will." Ben looked down at the commlink and smiled.

He looked up and found himself face-to-face with the Mole Man.

"Grimm," he said, and smacked Ben with a broom. "Grimm, Ben Grimm, Ben Grimm. Attack him, my subterraneans! Seize him! Rip him to shreds!"

The Mole Man—or Dr. Molekevic, as he was known back in the day when his brain was functional—wore a pale green hospital gown and dark sunglasses. He cackled to himself over and over, as he kept smacking Ben with the broom.

"That for destroying my underground fortress!" he said. "That for killing my creations! Attack, my subterraneans! Attack, attack, attack!"

There were, of course, no subterraneans. Ben let the poor man hit him a few times before grabbing his broom away and putting him in a headlock.

"Reed."

"Right here, Ben."

"I've got Molekevic. I want to stash him someplace safe. Any guards around, or—"

"Hold on."

Molekevic squirmed futilely, trying to get away.

"My subterraneans! To me!"

"Okay," Reed said. "There should be a brick building to your left."

Ben squinted through the smoke. "Yeah. I see it."

"That's the adolescent detention center. There ought to be plenty of guards in there."

There were; it took some talking on Ben's part, though, to get them even to open the door, and even more to take Molekevic into custody. The man was still going on about his subterraneans as Ben left.

He was halfway across the island when there was another explosion.

The ground shook.

The commlink buzzed.

"Reed."

"Ben. I'm tied in to the Con Ed video feed. That explosion you just heard?"

"That explosion I just felt, you mean. Some kind of storage tank?"

"Right. The second of three that feed the island's generator. Video feed shows me two Diablos trying to blow the third; a handful of security guards trying to hold them off."

"Two Diablos," Ben said. "Great."

"Ben. They blow the third tank, the generator goes down, the force shield goes down, and Building Twelve's psych ward residents become New York State residents."

"Great," Ben said. "Where's Yates?"

"I'm still looking for him."

"So where do I go?"

Reed told him. Ben broke into a jog; five minutes later, he was in front of the generator building, a big concrete blockhouse. There was no door. There was shouting and gunfire coming from inside.

"First door on your right inside is a stairwell, you go down two levels, then into the main power core," Reed said. "One of the Diablos is there, fighting the guards. I've lost track of the other one."

"Roger that," Ben said. "I'm going in."

"One more thing—big concrete building like that, I'm likely to lose the commlink signal once you're inside."

Ben nodded and headed through the front entrance before Reed could tell him what else might go wrong.

There was no door on his right, but he found the stairwell easily enough.

One flight down, he found the other Diablo as well, smiling and waiting for him.

"Señor Grimm," he said. "A pleasure to see you again."

"Wish I could say the same." Ben studied the thing in front of him; it sure looked like the real Diablo. He wished he knew what exactly a magical duplicate was, what it could do.

Only one way of finding out, he decided.

He took a swing at it. His fist passed through.

"You don't even know what I want," the Diablo said. "And yet you attack."

"Yeah. Guess I'm funny that way." Ben backed off. The Diablo advanced.

Okay, he thought. *It's kind of like a hologram—the magical version of a hologram, anyway. Sorcery, not science.*

He remembered something else Strange had told him about sorcery.

"It's illusion," Strange had said. "The threat appears as one thing when, in fact, it's another entirely."

The thing before him looked like Diablo, but it wasn't. So what was it? Some kind of energy, clearly. A lot like Reed's hologram, in fact, which his friend controlled remotely.

"I'm inclined not to hurt you, of course," the duplicate said. "Considering our history together. But . . ."

The Diablo raised its arms and gestured.

The stair railing next to him came to life, like some giant, metallic snake. Ben took a step back from it, and it shot out toward him, wrapping itself around his right arm before he could move. He grabbed it with his left; it whipped itself around the lower half of his body and began to squeeze.

The Diablo laughed.

Ben grunted and managed to turn his right hand enough to get a grip on the thing. Now he had it with both hands; he twisted. Something made an unholy shriek.

Ben kept twisting.

The creature snapped, and suddenly it was no longer a snake, it was just metal, metal that fell in bits to the ground.

He looked up. The Diablo was no longer smiling.

Just energy, Ben thought. *It's just energy,* and he knew how to deal with energy.

"Chaos approaches," the Diablo said. "You do not see it for what it is, but chaos approaches."

"I got an idea," Ben said. "Shut up."

He picked up a piece of the metal railing and thrust it through the creature.

The Diablo looked down and frowned.

"I do not know what your intent was, Señor Grimm," it said, "but that . . . that does nothing to me."

"Try this, then," Ben growled, and with his other hand, he ripped the power line from the wall and touched the sparking end of the torn wire to the metal rail.

For a second, his body thrummed with however many thousands of volts were in the line; Ben gritted his teeth and held on. He could handle that power, at least for the split second it took for the circuit breakers to kick in.

The Diablo, he was betting, couldn't.

The image wavered and disappeared.

The circuit breaker kicked in, and the lights in the stairwell flickered and went out. A second later, they kicked back on. Ben pushed through the door at the bottom of the stairs.

"Freeze!"

He found himself face-to-face with two security guards, guns drawn.

"It's all right. I'm one of the good guys." He looked past them. "Where's the other one?"

"The other what?" one of the guards said, lowering his weapon.

"The other Diablo."

"The thing we were fighting, you mean." The guard shook his head. "I don't know where it went. One second it was zapping us, and the next . . . it just disappeared."

Probably right when I zapped the one I was fighting, Ben

thought. What he'd done must have affected the real Diablo, wherever he was, his ability to maintain the duplicates.

There were more guards in the power core, some of them hurt. Ben helped the injured ones outside and got back on the commlink with Reed, who managed to get through to the Rikers hospital, get them to send out an ambulance.

"Nothing from Yates yet?" Ben asked.

"No."

"That's not good." Yates's call had come in, what, half an hour ago? For him not to make contact again in the interim . . .

"I have visual on Building Twelve now," Reed said. "Not a lot of activity going on there."

"That's not good, either."

"No."

Ben heard the wail of an ambulance in the distance. Through the smoke, he saw a red flashing light approaching. The guards roused themselves and began waving to it.

Ben looked north again, where the smoke was thickest. Building Twelve.

He put his head down and started running.

He hadn't gone more than a few hundred feet when a monster appeared out of the smoke in front of him. A demon. Purple-skinned, forked tail, horns . . .

The thing looked up at him and snarled.

"Desmond?" Ben said.

The demon's face changed.

"Ben?" it said. "Ben Grimm?"

"Yeah, buddy," Ben said. "It's me. Just take it easy, and . . ."

The demon stumbled forward.

One whole side of its body was charred and still smoking.

Yates, Ben thought, and this time, he wasn't just annoyed with the Torch, he was angry. No, beyond angry. He was beyond reason.

The demon was—had been—Desmond Pitt. An army buddy of Ben's. Pitt had been killed in a training accident.

He'd been resurrected by Doctor Doom—brought back from hell, his body reshaped into the form of a demon. Desmond's mind, unfortunately, had never quite completed the trip.

Ben lifted the demon's arm up around his shoulders and turned back the way he'd come. Toward the ambulance.

His friend was mumbling to himself.

"Chaos is coming, Ben. Death, and destruction, and the end of everything."

"I know, buddy, I know. You just take it easy." Desmond was talking just like Diablo; he wondered if the wizard had somehow seized control of him, too. Made him fight the Torch. Maybe that was why Yates had attacked Desmond. Maybe.

Ben would find out.

The hospital had sent two ambulances, two EMT crews. Their eyes widened when they saw Ben, and who—what—he was carrying.

Ben set Desmond on the ground and waved one of the crews over. He had to wave twice; they looked very reluctant to approach.

"What the . . ." one of the EMTs said.

"This is a friend of mine."

"This is a Building Twelve guy, isn't it?"

"Yeah. Not his fault, though, understand? I want you to help him. Make him comfortable."

One of the EMTs looked hesitant; the other stepped past him and knelt down next to Pitt. He took vitals, then looked up and shook his head.

"This guy's dead, Mr. Grimm."

Ben sighed. "I know. Do what you can."

The EMT frowned. "I don't understand. Do what I can?"

Desmond moaned again.

". . . destruction," he said. "Armageddon, apocalypse, doomsday. Chaos will reign . . ."

The EMT's jaw dropped.

Ben almost smiled.

"He's a demon, all right? Forget the vitals. See to the burns."

And off the EMT's slightly confused nod, Ben headed north again.

8

THE SMOKE, ODDLY ENOUGH, WAS DISSIPATING. Building Twelve—a squat concrete tower with attached, shorter structures to its left and right—looked calm. It looked as if nothing much was happening.

Ben slowed as he neared the main entrance.

"Reed."

"Right here."

"I'm outside Twelve."

"I see you. Psych ward is in the west wing—to your left."

Ben looked in that direction and saw a gaping hole in the side of the building.

"Yeah," he said. "I see it. Nothing from Yates?"

"Not yet."

"Where is the guy?"

"Believe me," Reed said, "you'll know the second I hear from him."

An orange-red rocket burst out of the hole in the building, shot past Ben, and slammed into the ground.

Yates got to his feet and swayed there a second.

"Think I found our man," Ben said.

Yates turned at the sound of his voice.

"About time you got here."

"What's going on?" Ben asked. "Why didn't you use the commlink?"

Yates held up his arm. The commlink strap was still on his wrist, but the unit itself was missing.

He walked right past Ben then, back toward the building.

"Hey!" Ben yelled after him. "Wait a second. Let's work this . . ."

Yates burst into flame and disappeared inside.

". . . as a team," Ben finished.

He put his hands on his hips.

"Ben?" The comm crackled. "What happened to Yates?"

"That's what I'm going to go find out," he said, and headed in himself.

The smoke was still thick inside the building.

Ben pushed his way past a pile of rubble and into a corridor.

A few yards in, he heard the sound of laughter. He looked left, then right. Nothing.

He looked down and saw a woman in a green hospital gown, sitting cross-legged on the floor. She held something up in the air in front of her. An insect.

A spider.

"It is I, Doctor Octopus," she said. "Run and tell your master I have returned, more powerful than ever."

She set the spider on the ground. It ran for the wall.

She looked up and saw Ben.

"My arms," she said. "Tell me where you have hidden my arms, and I will let you live."

"I'll go look for them now." Ben put a hand on her shoulder and strode past.

The corridor curved as he went; he began to lose his bearings. He heard the sounds of fighting nearby, a lot of fighting, but couldn't find a way to get to the battle.

He hit the commlink.

"Reed?"

No response.

"Reed. Can you give me a fix on my location, tell me where I am so—"

All at once, there was a huge crash, and a body flew through the wall to his left, smashed into the wall on his right, and crumpled to the ground. Diablo.

An American flag pushed through the wall after him. Nope. Not a flag. A man wearing a flag.

Captain America.

He turned and saw Ben.

"Grimm," he said. "Your man is out of control."

The military man in Ben—what was left of him, anyway, the old reflexes—had to resist the urge to salute. It was always that way whenever he saw the captain.

"My man?" Ben echoed. "You mean Yates?"

"Exactly. He's out of control. Utilizing excessive force. Tell him to back off. We have the situation in hand at this point."

"We?" Ben said, about to ask who *we* was, when all of a sudden it started to rain.

Inside the building, it started to rain, which told Ben all he needed to know about who the *we* was.

The smoke cleared.

Captain America picked up Diablo—the real Diablo, Ben assumed—threw him over his shoulder, and walked through the wall, back into the room he'd come from. Ben followed.

It was a rec room of some sort—had been a rec room, anyway, a smashed TV was on the floor, an overturned pool table, chairs scattered everywhere . . .

And standing in the middle of it, the rest of the Avengers: Hawkeye, Thor, Iron Man, the Wasp . . .

Yates was there, too, standing off to the side, still flaming in the rain.

Thor raised his hammer, and the rain stopped.

"We'll handle the cleanup," Captain America announced.

Ben looked at Yates, who shrugged.

"Sure," he said. "All yours."

He headed toward the nearest door. Ben, nodding hello and goodbye at the same time to the captain's team, turned to follow.

"Grimm."

The captain's voice stopped him at the door.

"Keep your man under control."

"He's not my man," Ben said. "And last I checked, I don't report to you."

"He's a problem," Captain America said. "If you don't solve it, someone else will have to."

"Meaning us," Hawkeye said.

"Is that so?" Ben asked.

"Mind your place, Hawkeye," Captain America said, without turning his head.

"Sure, Cap. Just letting Grimm know what's what." He smiled and mocked drawing a bow. *"Pfftt,"* he said, letting the pretend arrow fly. "And out goes the Torch."

"Hawkeye." This time, the captain did turn around. "Back in line."

The archer saluted.

"Nice to see another big happy family," Ben said, turning again. "You all take care now."

He left the room, and the building, and went off in search of Yates.

Ben found him pacing outside, talking to himself.

"Don't start with me," he said to Ben. "I made a mistake. I admit it. Diablo. I looked at the records and saw he'd served with Diehl, so I thought maybe he'd have some light to shed on the situation. How Diehl got so powerful. I thought I could get him to talk, but he must've . . ."

"He suckered you into letting him out of his cell."

"He didn't sucker me," Yates said. "I had my eye on him every step of the way."

"Then when did he have time to make those duplicates, or whatever those things were?"

"He didn't," Yates said. "He had help, obviously."

"Help." Ben shook his head. "Like who?"

Yates stopped walking. He was silent a moment. "You know who," he said at last.

Ben rolled his eyes.

"For crying out loud," he said. "You think Doom was involved in this?"

"It fits," Yates said. "I think he had something to do with Diehl, too. The increase in powers we saw . . ."

Ben was speechless. This was what had happened after Elizabeth, too: everyone's first instinct after the tragedy was to blame Doom. It was some kind of attack, they all said; Doom trying to conquer America. A surprise blow, a cowardly blow. The military was on the verge of sending nukes, till Reed finally got through to the president and proved that they were all wrong, that Doom had nothing to do with it.

Yates hadn't wanted to listen to reason then, any more than he wanted to listen now.

But Ben had to make him listen.

"I hate to be the bearer of bad news, Yates, but these are the facts," he said. "Doom is over in Europe. Doom had nothing to do with Elizabeth. Doom had nothing to do with Building Twelve. This was your cock-up, plain and simple, and the sooner you . . ."

"Get off my back," Yates said.

"I'll get off your back when you wake the hell up."

Yates muttered something anatomically impossible under his breath and started walking away. Ben, remembering Desmond, remembering Diehl, even remembering what the captain had said, was suddenly furious.

He grabbed Yates by the arm and spun him around.

"Listen. For the last couple months, you have been nothing but a . . ."

Yates flamed on, all at once. Ben drew his hand back in the nick of time to prevent being burned.

"What the hell is wrong with you these days?"

"What the hell is wrong with me?" Yates jabbed a finger right in Ben's chest. A burning finger. "What the hell is the matter with everyone else? Can't you see? It's Doom, all of this. He's responsible for Elizabeth, he's responsible for Diablo . . ."

Ben slapped Yates's hand away, none too gently.

"Next time you touch me with that finger," he said, "you lose it."

"Really?" Yates smiled and flared white.

Ben had to take a step back from the heat.

"Come on, Grimm," Yates said, moving forward. "Let's see what you got."

He raised his hand. There was a fireball in it.

Certifiable, Ben thought. *He's as certifiable as any of the loonies in Building Twelve.*

"What I got?" Ben said, continuing to back up. "This is what I got for you."

He brought his hands forward and clapped them together, hard as he could. There was a sudden *whoosh* of air and a sound like a thunderclap.

Yates's flame flickered for a second.

Ben's arm shot forward; he grabbed the man's throat with his right hand and squeezed.

"Flame on," he said, "and I'll snap your neck."

Yates sneered. "Do it, then. We'll go out together. A real blaze of glory, what do you say? You and me, buddy. Teammates. Comrades-in-arms, hey, Ben? What do you say?"

Ben looked the man in the eye and didn't know what to say. Damned if he didn't look serious.

"Come on, Ben," Yates said again. "Let's do it. What have we got to live for, anyway?"

"We got plenty to live for, genius. You got people who do think you're a hero, for one thing. Kids who look up to you. And you got kids of your own, dummy. You got a wife, you got . . ."

Yates started laughing.

"What the hell's so funny?" Ben asked.

Yates shook his head. "A wife. A wife." He laughed even harder.

Ben let go of him and stepped back.

"I don't know what's going on with you," he began, "but I think you better get your head straight before—"

"THAT'S RIGHT, YOU DON'T KNOW WHAT'S GOING ON WITH ME!" Yates shouted, and suddenly burst into flame. "YOU DON'T KNOW ANYTHING!"

Yates flared white-hot for a second again.

And then he went even hotter.

They were a few hundred yards from Building Twelve, standing on a concrete sidewalk, flanked by two rows of trees. Young trees, maybe fifteen, twenty feet high. There were benches, green plastic ones, lining the walk, too.

The trees burst into flame, then blackened and shriveled to ash.

The benches bubbled and melted into slag.

The grass burst into flame, too, and then was suddenly gone.

Ben felt his own skin begin to burn, and he was as close to invulnerable as anybody on the planet.

"YATES!" he yelled. "TONY! FOR GOD'S SAKE, STOP, YOU'LL—"

The Torch's flame went out, just as suddenly as it had started. Yates sat down hard on the ground.

The commlink crackled.

"Ben? What's going on?" Reed asked. "I just picked up a sudden heat surge . . ."

"It's all right," Ben said. "It's under control. Stand by."

He looked at Yates, who just sat there on the bare, blackened earth, shaking his head.

"Wife," Yates said, and smiled. There was no joy in that smile, just as there had been no amusement in his laughter before. "I have two of them, you know. Had three, but just two now. Joy, my ex. Sharon, my soon-to-be ex."

"I'm sorry about that," Ben said, because he didn't know what else to say, and also to cover up his embarrassment, because he had no idea who this Sharon was. He and Yates, he realized, hadn't talked much beyond mission specifics for a good long while. Years, even.

"Don't be. She's a bloodsucker. Just like the one before her." He shook his head. "My daughter warned me, you know. Maddy. She was eight, Kyle was six when their mother and I separated. Eight years old, but the first time Joy came over, Maddy saw right through her. Never got along. Joy made me send Maddy to boarding school. She never forgave me."

Ben nodded, though he was having a hard time keeping track of who was who—Joy, Kyle, Maddy, Sharon . . .

"Never," Yates said again. "Amara warned me, but I wouldn't listen. I never listened."

Amara. Ben remembered her. She was Yates's first wife—they'd split up maybe a year or so after the accident. Ugly divorce.

"She fought me on everything, you know. After the accident. I got so mad . . . I left her with almost nothing. Another thing the kids never forgave me for." He shook his head. "Drove her right out of Manhattan. The only place she could afford an apartment was New Jersey, which was pretty damn funny, because she always used to hate Jersey. Just like me."

"Just like you," Ben said. "What part of Jersey?"

Yates looked up, and Ben knew then, even before he spoke.

"Roselle Park," Yates said. "Right outside Elizabeth."

"Oh." Ben didn't know what else to say.

Both men were silent a moment.

"I screwed up, Ben," Yates said. "I had everything, and I screwed it up so bad I don't even know where to start fixing it."

Ben shifted uncomfortably. He wished Alicia were there—she'd know how to talk to Yates. She'd know what to say to calm him down.

Of course, he reflected, she'd make him do the talking anyway. The same way she'd made him talk to Max last night. Fat lotta good that had done.

"Tony," he began. "All right. You messed up. But you can fix it. You apologize, and you start again."

"Amara's dead. I can't apologize to her."

"I'm talking about your kids."

Yates sighed. He didn't say anything for a minute, then he nodded.

"Yeah. Maybe you're right. Talk to the kids."

Yates started to get to his feet. Ben held out a hand and helped him up.

"Thanks," Yates said.

"You're welcome. Now let's get back to headquarters. You can make a call or two, and then maybe you can help me convince Reed—"

"I'll be there," Yates interrupted. "Soon."

And then, before Ben could respond, he flamed on and flew off up into the sky.

And then he was gone.

9

THE ROOF CANOPY ATOP THE BAXTER BUILDING opened, and Ben set the aerocar down. He walked down to C level and headed straight for medical.

Reed's hologram popped up in front of him.

"That was quite a conversation," it said.

"You eavesdropped."

"You had the commlink open."

"It was private." Ben reached the door to medical and tried the knob. Still locked.

"I apologize. But I'm glad I heard it. We're a team, Ben, even if we haven't been acting like it so much the last few months. It's important to know what's going on with each other."

"So true," he said. "So why don't you open this door, so I can see what's going on with you?"

The hologram shook its head.

"I'll be out in a few hours, Ben. When the treatment is over. I leave before that, there'll be complications."

Like what? Ben was about to ask, and then sighed. He didn't have another big fight in him just then.

"Okay. A few more hours. Nothing from Max yet?"

"No."

Ben turned and headed for the command center. "This is crazy. I'm going to call Rose."

"I just spoke with her."

"I'm calling my brother, then."

"That might not be the wisest course of action. Word could spread, and—"

"All right, all right." Ben plunked himself down in a chair. "So what do we do?"

"We wait."

"I'm not good at waiting. You tried the commlink, right? Maybe he was just out of range."

"I did."

"I'm going to try it again," he said, reached for the controls, and frowned.

There was a bank of security monitors in front of him—the one showing him Level A displayed not just the android fabrication facility but a tall, spider-thin old woman in an old-fashioned dress, surveying the room as if she owned it.

"Who's that? New cleaning lady?" Ben asked.

"Hardly. Her name is Harkness," Reed said. "Stephen suggested I call her."

Ben nodded. She looked the type, all right. Witchy.

"So what's she doing here?"

"Reviewing our defenses."

"Finding out what went wrong, hey?"

On the monitor, the woman turned and looked directly at Ben.

"Nothing went wrong," she said, and then disappeared.

"The intruder brought forces to bear we did not anticipate."

Ben almost jumped right out of his skin.

The woman was, all of a sudden, standing right in front of him.

Magicians, Ben thought. *Hate 'em.*

"Ben Grimm, Agatha Harkness," Reed said, making the introductions.

Ben stood. He came up about eye-level to her chest.

"Pleased to meet you." He held out a hand to shake; she frowned.

"I do not engage in unnecessary physical contact," she said. "It weakens my aura."

"Right," Ben said. "Well, we wouldn't want that."

She raised an eyebrow, then turned to Reed.

"I have as yet found nothing to dispel my initial impressions, Doctor Richards. The defenses Stephen put in place are still intact, as I said."

"Can you strengthen them? So that if Diehl returns . . ."

Harkness shook her head. "I do not have that kind of power."

"All right. Why don't you finish looking everything over, and we'll review our options then."

"As you wish," she said, and, just like that, disappeared from the room . . . and reappeared on the monitor.

Ben was about to make a joke about Old World charm, then remembered that Harkness had heard him before, when he spoke. Hard to tell, of course, after such a short meeting, but she didn't seem like the kind of woman with a great sense of humor.

He held the humor for later.

"So you think Diehl might come back?" he asked Reed.

"Yes."

"To destroy the Q-Ray."

"I'm not positive that was his intention."

"He sounded pretty positive about it to me."

"Part of the time, yes. But part of the time . . ." The hologram shook its head. "I've been looking at footage from the security cameras all morning. His mannerisms, his words, his actions . . . he seemed confused, more than anything else."

He wasn't the only one, Ben thought, thinking of the expression on his own face when Diehl had appeared. The expression he couldn't remember making.

"Well. If he doesn't want to destroy the Q-Ray . . ."

"He may want to use it."

"To build his own quantum computer?"

"That's one possibility."

"There are others, I assume."

"Yes."

Ben waited, but Reed didn't say anything else. Suddenly, he remembered that the two of them had been talking about just this subject when Yates's call had come through. What was the phrase Reed had used . . .

"Hilbert space," he recalled. "You were saying something about a Hilbert space?"

Reed nodded. "There is a possibility—with a certain degree of reprogramming—that the Q-Ray could be used to project an exclusionary Hilbert space."

"And that's a bad thing."

"Yes."

"How bad?"

"Very bad."

"A Baxter Building blowing up kind of bad, an H-bomb kind of bad . . ."

"Catastrophic," Reed said. "A no-more-Negative-Zone kind of bad."

Ben frowned. He didn't like the sound of that.

"So we destroy it. The Q-Ray, I mean."

Reed was silent a moment before speaking.

"Possibly."

"Why possibly? Why not definitely?"

The hologram hesitated before replying. "I have

some other . . . theories to explore, before I'm ready to commit to that course of action."

"Like what?"

Reed shook his head. "I'm not ready to say just now."

"You got a time frame on when you will be?"

"Soon," the hologram snapped. "I'm working as fast as I can."

Ben recognized that tone in Reed's voice. He wouldn't be rushed.

"Okay. But sounds to me like we're taking an awful risk here. If Diehl comes back . . ."

"We'll be ready for him this time," Reed said. "All four of us."

"Four of us?" Ben made a point of looking around the room. "I don't see four of us here, Reed. I see me, and I sort of see you. So that makes—let's see—the Fantastic One and a Half, let's call it. Unless you want to count the old woman."

On the monitor, Harkness turned and frowned at him.

The phone chirped.

"You ask me, we ought to destroy it," Ben said, and picked up the receiver. "Grimm here."

"Mister Grimm." It was one of the O'Hoolihans downstairs, at the security desk. "You have a visitor."

"A visitor?" Ben looked over at the monitor that showed the picture from the desk.

Johnny Storm waved up at him.

"Big Ben."

"Little John." Ben smiled in spite of himself.

Johnny smiled, too. "What's the matter, I'm not good enough for you to return my phone calls?"

Ben was on the verge of a snappy comeback when he saw that the O'Hoolihan droid was wrong. It wasn't just one visitor he had—it was two.

Behind Johnny stood his sister.

"Sue," Ben said.

He glanced reflexively over his shoulder.

The Reed hologram, as he expected, wasn't there anymore.

He left the command center, went to visitor access. Johnny walked off the elevator first; he and Ben shook hands, clapped each other on the back.

"Good to see you, kid," Ben said.

Johnny opened his mouth to reply, and Ben stepped right past him to Sue.

The two of them embraced.

When she stepped back, there were tears in her eyes.

"Ben," she said. "Tell me it hasn't really been ten years."

"It hasn't," he said. "We went through some kind of time warp, obviously."

She smiled. "There are no time warps in my life, Ben. That's you."

"Ahhh . . . I don't know about that. Time warp's the

only explanation I can figure. 'Cause you look exactly the same."

"Liar. But it's nice to hear anyway."

"I'm not lying, Suzy." And he wasn't; he couldn't see any difference between the Sue Storm he'd last seen the day before the launch and the Sue who stood in front of him now. Okay, maybe the hairstyle. She wasn't wearing it long anymore; she had it up off her shoulders. And the clothes; the Sue in front of him now had on a business suit; back then she was a med student, always in jeans and whatever shirt she could find. Usually one of Reed's.

"I saw in the papers," Sue said. "You're married."

He nodded. "Eight years now." He felt a pang of guilt then; he'd wanted Sue at the wedding, Johnny, too, but after what had happened . . . it just didn't seem like a good idea. "We got kids, too. Hold on."

He went to the reception desk and brought up a few pictures he'd put in the system. Then he spun the display around so Sue and Johnny could see.

"They're beautiful," she said. "How old?"

"Six and five."

"Must've been the mailman," Johnny said.

"Har-har." Ben spun the display back around. "So what's going on with you two these days? What brings you to town?"

"I got a few meetings," Johnny said. "Top-secret stuff."

"Right." Ben smiled. "Really. What's going on?"

"I'm serious," Johnny said.

"He's not lying, Ben." Sue put a hand on her brother's shoulder and smiled. "Tomorrow morning, nine-thirty at the Federal Building, two S.H.I.E.L.D. agents, a NASA scientist, and an undersecretary of defense will be the first to witness a presentation by one Jonathan Lowell Spencer Storm on a revolutionary new personal transportation vehicle, one that—"

"Whoa, whoa, Sue." Johnny held up a hand to stop his sister. "Seriously. This is top-secret stuff. We're really not supposed to talk about it."

Ben was dumbfounded.

"You really . . ." He shook his head and looked at Johnny and Sue. "Top-secret, huh? Hold on a minute."

He went quickly to his quarters, got his S.H.I.E.L.D. ID, and brought it back to Johnny.

"Here," he said. "Now, tell me about this thing."

Johnny made a show of frowning. "Hold on a minute." He held up the ID and looked from it to Ben. "I guess it's you. What do you think, Sue?"

"Johnny." She rolled her eyes. "Will you stop fooling around for one minute, please, and tell Ben what you've done?"

"Well." Johnny handed Ben back the ID. "You remember that company Wyatt and I started?"

"Wyatt?" He frowned, then snapped his fingers. "Wingfoot, right? The football player?"

"One and the same."

"I didn't know you guys started a company."

"Internet thing—place to buy used high-end cars. Performance cars?"

"Oh, yeah," Ben said.

"We made a couple million off that, and then—"

"You made a couple million dollars."

"Yeah."

Ben frowned and looked Johnny over again. He was wearing jeans and a T-shirt that said "Storm the Internet." Nice-enough-looking jeans, nice-enough-looking shirt . . .

He did have on really nice leather shoes. Those had to be a few hundred bucks.

And a ring on one hand, with a shiny stone in it. It couldn't be a diamond, though; it was way too big to be a diamond. Alicia's diamond wasn't that big.

"What are you looking at?" Johnny asked.

"You," Ben said, and smiled. "Johnny Storm, boy millionaire."

"What—you didn't think I had it in me?"

Johnny smiled then, too, and talked more about the company he and Wyatt had started. Then he talked about the personal transport vehicle he was demonstrating tomorrow. Some kind of high-performance engine, small enough—and energy-efficient enough—to make a one-person car practical. Ben was half listening, half shaking his head in admiration.

He hadn't always thought Johnny had it in him, to be honest. He always liked the kid—not a bad bone in his body, just a bit of a hot dog, especially when he got up in the air. He was happy to find Johnny grounded, to find that there was, after all, a little substance behind all the flash.

And then Johnny stopped talking, and Ben found himself looking at Sue once more.

"And what about you?" he asked. "You still in Dallas?"

She laughed. "Dallas? I left Dallas a long time ago. No, I'm in LA now."

"LA? You?" Ben shook his head. "I don't see it. Sue Storm, doctor to the stars?"

"Not really. I run a genetics clinic in Inglewood."

"Ah." Ben nodded. That he could see.

And how's your love life? he almost asked, but suspected he knew the answer already. The first thing he'd looked at when Sue had come off the elevator was her left hand. No rings there. No jewelry at all.

"Ben," she said. "Where's Reed?"

He cleared his throat.

"Ah. Reed. Well, the thing of it is, he's out on a mission. Should be back soon, if you want to wait. Or I have your number, Johnny, I could have him call and—"

"You are still—after all this time—a terrible liar. He doesn't want to see me." Sue smiled—with her mouth, at least. Her eyes held an entirely different expression. "That's all right. I knew this was a . . . a bad idea. But I wanted to see you, too. It has been too long."

"No, that's not it, Suzy," Ben blurted out. "Reed's sick. He's in the medical lab."

The second the words were out of his mouth, Ben kicked himself for saying them, for telling her the truth. Ten years on, and he still couldn't lie to Sue Storm.

"Sick?" Sue frowned. "It doesn't have anything to do with what happened to him at Elizabeth, does it?"

"No. This is a totally different thing." Then it was Ben's turn to frown. "Hey? How do you know about Elizabeth?"

"I know every geneticist on the East Coast. Every lab supervisor, every radiation specialist. And Elizabeth made headlines in every paper—even *Variety.* I made it my business to find out. Even if he doesn't . . ." She made an expression of disgust. "Oh, it doesn't matter. What's the matter with him now?"

"Nothing major," Ben said. "It's under control."

"Under control." She gave Ben that same penetrating look again. "What is it?"

Ben stammered.

"What does his doctor say?"

Ben stammered again.

"He doesn't have a doctor." Sue shook her head. "He's treating himself."

"Yeah, but . . . Max looked at the machines," Ben offered. "He said it was all right."

Sue tapped her foot.

"Basically," Ben added.

"Max. He and Reed are two peas in a pod, Ben, you know that. They'd forget to eat if you weren't around to remind them. Am I right?"

Remembering what had happened yesterday, Ben could only nod.

"So what exactly is wrong?"

"I guess I'm not entirely sure. It was when he went into the Negative Zone," Ben said. "He had to go into the decontamination chamber."

"Decontamination chamber?" Sue's eyes widened.

"Negative Zone?" Johnny laughed. "You're kidding me. There's a place called the Negative Zone? Tell me that there's not like a Negative Spider-Man in there. A Negative Hulk, a Negative Thor—"

"Johnny," Sue snapped. "Hush, Ben, is this radiation sickness he has?"

"I think so, but—"

"Where is he?" She looked over Ben's shoulder, toward the door at the far end of the room, the one that led into the staging area, where they'd held the abortive Q-Ray computer demonstration yesterday. "In there?"

"No," Ben said. "Upstairs."

"Take me to him," Sue said.

Ben shook his head. "Sue. In the first place—"

"Ben Grimm." She folded her hands across her chest. "Ten years ago, you were a fairly intelligent man. Tell me that along with getting ridiculously strong, you haven't gotten ridiculously stupid, too."

"No, I like to think—"

"Because you know that after Elizabeth—on top of what happened to the four of you ten years ago—Reed Richards is lucky to be alive. Lucky not to be a bowl of primordial DNA soup. Radiation messed up his genetic structure, and if he's gotten himself exposed to radiation again, he needs to be treated by a competent medical professional immediately. How long has it been since this Negative Zone incident?"

"A day," Ben said.

"A day." Sue shook her head. "Take me to him."

"I can't . . ."

"Fine. I'll find him myself." She strode toward the far door.

"Sue," Ben called after her. "We got a rule. No civilians allowed . . ."

She went through the door.

". . . in the command center," he finished.

He shook his head and started after her; Johnny was a step behind him.

"Hey, relax," Johnny said. "She does that sort of thing to me all the time."

He caught up to her in the next room. She was studying all the monitors.

"I see a door that says 'Medical,' " she said, pointing to one of the screens. "How do I get to it?"

"You don't," Ben said. "Really, Sue. You can't be in here."

She didn't even look up. "Let's put that on Reed's

tombstone, shall we? Here lies Reed Richards, or what's left of him, at least, saved from having to see a doctor at the last by his good friend, Benjamin J. Grimm."

Ben sighed. "All right, all right. Here's what I'll do."

Sue looked up.

"I'll go talk to him. I'll see if he'll agree . . ."

"Ben, for God's sake." Sue shook her head. "Reed doesn't get a choice in this."

"He's locked himself in, Suzy," Ben said. "I have to convince him . . ."

"There?" She pointed at the monitor that showed the Level C corridor, just outside medical. "He's locked in there?"

"Yeah, but Sue . . ."

"All right," she said. "Let's go."

The commlink sounded.

Johnny and Sue looked at each other.

"Excuse me," Ben said, and stepped past them to open the circuit. The nearest monitor went dark for a second and then came back to life.

It was Max.

He looked as if he hadn't slept at all. His uniform was rumpled. There was stubble on his face. His hair was a matted, tangled mess.

"Game nineteen, Ben," he said. "I wonder if I could replay that last move I made."

"Max?" Ben leaned in closer. "Are you all right?"

His friend shook his head. "No. It occurred to me,

though, that I wanted to replay one of the moves from last night. If you'd allow me."

"Where are you?" Ben asked.

"I'm home," he said. "Though it still doesn't feel like home to me. It doesn't feel right, Ben—does that make any sense? It doesn't . . ."

The commlink was a two-way audio and visual; it let Ben see and hear Max, it let Max see and hear him, and whoever else was in the command center.

His voice trailed off as he looked over Ben's shoulder and saw Sue and Johnny.

"I know you," he said.

Sue responded first. "Yes. Sue Storm—my brother, Johnny. We met before the Mars flight . . . ?"

"Of course. I remember." He frowned and looked at Ben. "They're your friends, Ben, but . . ."

"I know, I know," Ben said. "No civilians in the command center. Just let me call you right back, okay?"

"Okay," Max said.

Ben closed the circuit.

"What's the matter with him?" Sue asked.

"I don't know that, either, and before you start in with me, I'm trying my damnedest to find out, okay?"

"Of course," Sue said.

"You guys seem to be having some problems around here," Johnny said.

"You don't know the half of it," Ben said.

"Where's the other guy? The Torch?"

"Don't even start," Ben said. "Listen, I'm going to call Reed—just to tell him we're on the way up, okay?"

Without waiting for a response, he reached for the screen control that would patch him through to medical, though he was ninety-nine-and-ninety-nine-one-hundredths-percent certain that Reed had been listening to every word they'd just said.

He touched the screen—

And a hand reached out of the monitor and grabbed his.

Sue screamed.

"Whoa," Johnny said, and stumbled backward.

The hand pulled on his, and an arm, and then a shoulder, and then a head followed it through the monitor.

Ben found himself looking into the Harkness woman's face.

"Help," she croaked, and there were tears on her face, and there was pain—no, agony—in her voice "Please help. I—"

Something yanked her backward then, and her eyes widened and rolled back in her head.

That something began to pull her back through the monitor.

Ben decided not to let it.

He yanked back. It was a tug-of-war for a second.

Somebody laughed.

Ben looked up; his eyes went to the row of security monitors.

Jembay Diehl's face was on every one.

"The woman is mine," he said, and then there was a tug that Ben couldn't resist, and the Harkness woman was gone, just like that.

And Diehl was in the command center with them, holding her lifeless body by the hair.

"Her, and her power," the magician said, and then folded Harkness in half, and in half again, and a third time, and then he held up what was left of her, a little sphere of glowing light no bigger than a baseball, and popped it into his mouth.

"Oh, man," Johnny said. "Tell me that did not just happen. Ben, tell me . . ."

"I want the machine," Diehl said. "Where is it?"

Ben stepped forward, placing himself in front of Sue and Johnny.

"Over my dead body," he said.

Diehl smiled again. "As you wish," he said, and raised his arms to strike.

10

NO CIVILIANS IN THE COMMAND CENTER, BEN told himself. *We have rules, and there are reasons we have rules, because of crazy, wacky things like this, like lunatic sorcerers popping up out of computer screens, and folding old ladies lengthwise three times and then swallowing them whole.*

An alarm sounded. The elevator door—the only other way in or out of the command center—slid open. A car full of O'Hoolihans, half a dozen at least, started forward, weapons coming to bear as they moved.

Diehl waved a hand, and the elevator was suddenly gone, and where it had been was a wall. Hands—and some feet—stuck out of the wall, still holding weapons, wiggling futilely in the air.

Ben used the instant of distraction to start forward.

Red fire exploded from Diehl's fingertips.

Bolts of energy slammed into Ben's chest.

He staggered backward.

Sue and Johnny caught him.

"The machine," Diehl said. "Where is it?"

No confusion in his eyes now. No talk of destroying the Q-Ray to prevent it from being used. Diehl, Ben thought, looked—and sounded—like an entirely different person. A much more powerful person, if that last energy blast was anything to go by.

"No civilians in the command center," Ben said, and put his hands together over his head into a single fist and slammed them down on the floor.

He heard Johnny and Sue exclaim behind him, and stumble, but he couldn't worry about that right now. Diehl stumbled, too, and that was what Ben was after, and as the magician righted himself, Ben was already on him, drawing his right fist back for a haymaker that would put a quick end to this fight, clobberin' time, clobberin' time, clobberin' time, and his arm shot forward, and his fist, half an inch from Diehl's jaw, suddenly was stuck in a wall of marshmallow a foot thick.

At least, that's what it felt like.

What it looked like was a soft yellow light, entirely surrounding his hand.

The magician smiled.

The light began to contract around Ben's fingers. He tried to draw his hand away but couldn't.

The light began to squeeze.

Ben gritted his teeth. Hurt like a sonuvagun. One time he had arm-wrestled the Hulk, just for the heck of it, one time when Banner's mind had control of the Hulk's body. That match was pretty much over in that first instant when he and Banner had locked hands and he'd felt the strength behind the other man's grip. Ben was surprised when the match lasted ten seconds—afterward, he had the feeling that Banner had held back, out of some sense of graciousness, or as a salve to Ben's own pride.

The light was stronger. Much stronger.

And Diehl had no intention of holding back.

"The Q-Ray," Diehl said. "Where?"

"Even if I knew," Ben said, "don't know as I'd tell you."

The light squeezed again.

Ben heard a crack.

"Oh, God," he heard Sue say, and something red ran down the back of his hand.

Blood. His blood.

Ben hadn't bled since the accident. The press called him Mr. Invulnerable, and Reed said the name fit, that he really was as close to invulnerable as anyone could get. Reed said that. And Reed was right, Reed was always right, wasn't he?

Ben realized he was screaming. He bit down on his tongue to stop and tasted his blood.

"Hey, you looking for a machine?"

That was Johnny. Ben had no idea what he was doing, but . . .

"Get out of here, Johnny!" he yelled. "Take Sue, and get out the way you came!"

"Sue," Johnny said. "Toss me that little gizmo out of your pocketbook, would you?"

Ben turned. He couldn't get his head all the way around, but out of the corner of his eye, he saw Sue doing just that, handing Johnny something metallic, cylindrical, about the size of a lipstick.

"My version of a taser," Johnny said. "Uses a modified version of the PTV engine, not that you know what I'm talking about, but the point is, it delivers a lot more energy over a sustained period of time. Not really for use against humans, but then, you're not really human, are you?"

Diehl wasn't even listening. He was focused entirely on Ben. All to the good.

"Johnny!" Ben yelled again. "You get out of here, you stupid—"

"I will take your hand off," Diehl said to Ben. "And then I will take the rest of the arm, and then a leg, and then I'll do it again until you tell me where the Q-Ray is."

Ben gasped in pain.

He heard footsteps coming up behind him.

"Here," Johnny said. "See what I mean."

"Johnny, for crying out loud," Ben said. "This is not some stupid game. Take Sue and . . ."

Something flew past Ben then and landed on Diehl.

The magician looked down. Ben saw a thin line of wire leading back from Diehl to—

"Try this," Johnny said, and the wire lit up for a second, glowing blue-white with power. Ben could feel the air sizzle with energy.

Diehl blinked, and his gaze shifted from Ben to someplace behind Ben. To Johnny.

"You try it," Diehl said, and suddenly the wire burst into flame and blackened.

And Sue screamed.

"JOHNNY!"

Ben turned his head as far as he could.

Far enough to see Johnny Storm was on fire.

Another alarm sounded, the fire alarm, and sprinklers shot down from the roof and began to spray foam.

And then stopped.

Diehl smiled.

"Bubble, bubble," he said. "Fire burn, and flesh bubble."

Not enough foam had reached the flames to douse them: Johnny was screaming now.

Ben cursed and put his left hand on his right arm and began to pull with that, too. He heard another crack; he didn't care. He pulled and pulled, and screamed and screamed.

No civilians in the command center, Ben thought. *No civilians. There are rules, and there are reasons for rules, and . . .*

"By your reaction, I judge these to be friends of yours," Diehl said.

Ben didn't respond.

Diehl waved a hand, and suddenly Sue was floating in the air, right in front of Ben. She was in a bubble of some kind, a bubble made up of the same yellow light that surrounded Ben's hand.

She was shaking her head and trying to speak. No. Trying to breathe.

There was no air in the bubble.

"It's a vacuum," Diehl said. "I don't suppose she has much more than five seconds to live. Unless—"

"NO!" Ben shouted. "I DON'T KNOW WHERE IT IS!"

"Five," Diehl said. "Four."

"I'M TELLING THE TRUTH, I DON'T KNOW—"

"Three—"

Diehl never got the whole number out.

A rope shot through the air toward him, and on the end of that rope was a fist, and the fist hit Diehl square in the face.

The man staggered back, and the fist hit him again. Diehl backed up, and the rope followed, and Ben saw that it wasn't a rope, it was Reed's arm, and coming through the door right behind it was Reed himself.

And Ben had never, ever seen a look on his friend's face like he saw now.

Diehl raised his arms to strike back. Reed's other arm shot around behind him and pulled the man's legs out from under him. Diehl hit the floor with a crash, face-first, and groaned, and rolled over. Blood was coming from the corner of the man's mouth.

And Reed hit him again.

Reed was wearing gloves of some sort, Ben saw now. They looked like some kind of chain mail—metallic gold. They caught the light as they flew through the air, hitting over and over again.

The pressure around Ben's fist was suddenly gone—he could move his hand, and for a split second that was a relief, and then he felt the pain full-on and staggered where he stood.

Through the fog of that pain, he realized that if the light around his hand was gone, the light around Sue—

He looked up in time to see her fall and Reed catch her.

Reed pulled the gloves off and fell to his knees next to Sue. He brushed her hair back from her face.

"Sue," he said gently. "Please wake up. Sue . . ."

Her eyes fluttered and opened.

"Reed," she said, and smiled, and then her eyes shot open. "Johnny . . ."

Ben was already at her brother's side.

He was burned all over, his skin cracked and blackened and oozing.

His eyes were wide open.

Breath rattled in his throat.

"Oh, God," Ben said. "He's still alive."

Reed punched a button on his wrist comm. "Stretcher to command center, Priority One-A," he said, helping Sue to her feet.

"You're all right?"

"I'm all right," she said. "Never mind about me. Johnny—"

"We'll get him up to medical quick as we can."

"You have plasma?" Sue asked.

"We have everything," Reed said.

"What about Diehl?" Ben asked. "We can't just leave him here. He might wake up and . . ."

"Bring him, too. Put him in Lab Three," Reed said. "I'll take care of him later."

"Lab Three," Ben said, and at that second, two Robertas came running into the room, one with a stretcher.

"Here," Ben said, and helped them gently lift Johnny onto it with his one good hand.

"Let's go," Reed said. "On the double."

They went.

Sue and Reed stood over her brother, working feverishly. Ben watched through the observation glass, as one of the Roberta droids worked on his hand, putting it in a cast. Ben shook his head. Mr. Invulnerable in a cast. It didn't seem right.

Sue looked cool as a cucumber—just another day at the office, never mind the fact that she was standing next to her onetime fiancé for the first time in a decade or that it was her half-dead brother she was operating on. Unbelievable. Ben didn't even want to think about his mental state if somebody hurt Dan. Or, God forbid, Alicia.

And the kids . . .

Magic, he thought. He hated magic.

He thought about Diehl then, still unconscious down the hall in Lab 3, unconscious and lying in the middle of a circle that Reed had drawn around him a few minutes ago, drawn with a pink stick of chalk.

"You gotta be kidding," Ben had said, watching in disbelief.

"No."

"The chalk is going to keep him from attacking us again."

"The chalk confines him," Reed said. "Confines his powers inside it. It's special chalk."

"Must be."

"Stephen had it sent over."

"The same Stephen who magic-proofed the building in the first place?"

"That's right. The same Stephen who sent over the gloves."

"Oh," was all Ben could say to that. He'd gotten a better look at those gloves after they'd come upstairs; they were made of some kind of chain mail, only it felt soft as silk when Ben had touched them. There was writing all over them, weird little symbols of some sort. Runes, Reed had called them. They were special gloves, all right. So maybe this chalk . . .

Yates strode into medical.

"Ben?" He looked at the cast and frowned.

"You're hurt."

"Yes."

"You. Are hurt."

"There's a first time for everything."

"What happened?" He looked into the operating theater. "What's going on? Is that Sue Storm?"

"Uh-huh. And Johnny." He filled Yates in on everything that had happened.

"Chalk?" Yates said.

"Uh-huh. Special chalk, Reed said."

"It had better be." The man frowned. "I'm going to go see for myself."

He came back a few seconds later, just as the Roberta sealed Ben's cast.

"Don't get it wet," the android said. "Don't put it in water. Don't—"

"He's awake," Yates said. "Diehl. And believe it or not, I think the chalk is working."

Ben followed Yates down the hall to Lab 3. Diehl was indeed awake—awake and pacing inside the pink circle. The look on his face was something to behold.

Ben smiled. "Let me guess. Pink is not your favorite color."

Diehl didn't respond.

Reed walked into the room.

"How's the kid?" Ben asked. "Johnny?"

"Critical," Reed said, peeling off his medical coverall. "The next couple of hours will tell the story."

"And Sue? How's she holding up?"

"More worried about him than anything else. Ben." Reed looked him in the eye. "We have a rule, and there's a reason we have that rule. No civilians in the command center. Because you didn't follow that rule, we have—"

"I know," Ben said. "Listen, you got every right to be mad at me, but you can't possibly be as angry as I am at myself. Believe me."

"I don't know about that," Reed said. "I'm fairly angry."

"Be angry at me, then. Not Ben."

All three of them—Reed, Yates, Ben—turned toward the door to the access corridor, where Sue stood, a white coverall over the business suit she'd been wearing.

"I broke the rule, Reed. Not Ben. And I broke it because I was concerned about you."

"Me?" Reed frowned. "Why . . ."

"Yes. You, Reed," Sue interrupted, and then explained what Ben had told her. "Johnny's as stable as I can get him for the moment, so I want you to come back to the medical lab and let me examine you. A real examination, not one of those machine scans you're so fond of."

"The medlab scanners are quite accurate," Reed said.

"I'm sure they are. I don't know how in the world they can know everything to scan for, but I'm sure they're quite accurate at what they do."

"I can't do it, Sue," he said. "Not right now."

"You don't get a choice."

"I need to find out what this man knows," Reed said.

"We need to find out how the Negative Zone radiation affected you."

"We will. As soon as—"

"Reed." Sue folded her arms across her chest. "This is a matter of life and death. Yours."

"And this is a matter of life and death as well," Reed said, nodding in Diehl's direction. "Only a lot more lives—potentially a lot more deaths—are involved."

She frowned.

Ben frowned, too.

All at once, looking at Reed and Sue standing there, facing off against each other, he had a feeling of déjà vu again, only this was déjà vu to the hundredth power, déjà vu as if he'd witnessed this kind of scene, this kind of argument, a hundred, a thousand times before.

"Reed," Yates said. "I think you'd better explain that last statement."

"All I have is a theory," Reed said. "I want to talk to Diehl before I decide whether or not it's worth sharing."

"But even if it is, you'll wait to share it. Till after I examine you," Sue said. "Right?"

Reed nodded. "Right. After you examine me."

"Thank you," she said. "I'll be with Johnny, then."

She and Reed exchanged a smile. Ben wouldn't have even seen it if he hadn't been watching Sue closely. In that second, though, he felt like an intruder—almost as if he was eavesdropping on a private conversation, because there was a lot more to that smile than mutual good wishes. It was a look fraught with meaning, the kind of look that only people who'd known each other for a long, long time could exchange, people who had a shared history, who could reduce that history to a single glance.

It was the kind of look he and Alicia sometimes shared, when they were stuck in a room full of strangers, or friends even, and unable to talk.

And with that thought, Ben felt again that terrible sense of unease that had come on him yesterday. He shook it off.

Sue left the room.

"She looks exactly the same," Yates said. "Whatever happened between you two, anyway? Why . . ."

Reed glared. "I don't think that's important just

now. Let's focus on the task in front of us, yes?"

Ben felt like reminding Reed of what he'd said earlier in the day—about them all being a team, about it being good to know what was going on in each other's lives. He didn't think that would get him much other than a glare of his own, so instead of talking, he stepped up to the pink chalk line and frowned.

"So what's the plan?" he asked, nodding to Diehl, who now stood with his back to them, facing the far wall.

"I have a few questions for our friend here," Reed said. "Ones I'm sure he'll be quite happy to answer."

"Going to put on the gloves, huh?" Ben said. "Let me. It'd be a pleasure."

"I don't think the gloves will be necessary," Reed said. "Mr. Diehl. How did you first learn of the Q-Ray?"

The man didn't move.

"You're not a scientist, Mr. Diehl. How did you come to realize that the Q-Ray could be used for purposes other than its original intent?"

Diehl remained silent.

So did Ben, though he began to see where Reed was going with this line of questioning. The exclusionary Hilbert space, if he was remembering the terminology right.

"A little hotfoot might loosen his tongue," Yates said.

"No, no." Reed shook his head.

"The gloves, then," Ben said. "I'll go get them."

"No." Reed took a piece of blue chalk from his pocket and smiled.

Ben looked at Yates, who shrugged.

This was getting weirder by the second.

Reed knelt down on the floor and began to draw with the chalk.

The second it touched the floor, Diehl spun and charged. He came so fast Ben flinched reflexively and braced himself for impact.

But it never came. An inch from the edge of the circle, Diehl slammed into something that knocked him backward as fast he'd come running. He fell to the floor.

Reed hadn't budged, hadn't even looked up.

"Don't smudge the chalk line," he said, and began to trace another circle with the blue crayon, around the edges of the pink one. He was careful, Ben saw, to make sure the two colors never actually touched.

"You're doing magic," Ben said. "How can you do magic?"

"Stephen and I discussed contingencies. This was one of them."

"Blue chalk." Ben shook his head and exchanged a look with Yates. Weird, and getting weirder, but whatever Reed was doing . . .

It seemed to be working.

Diehl paced back and forth inside the chalk circle, growing more and more agitated.

Reed continued drawing; Diehl got down on his hands and knees, too, and scrambled to the other side of the pink circle, as close to the edge as he could come, and began shouting. For a split second, Ben thought he was cursing, then realized he was using another language entirely, that Diehl, too, was doing magic.

Things—colors, shapes, creatures—of all kinds appeared in the air above him, growling, and hissing, and spitting at Reed, who ignored them all. None of the creatures could get past the chalk, either.

"When I finish this," Reed said calmly, "I'll ask my questions of you again, Mr. Diehl, and you, I understand, will be bound to answer."

Diehl screamed wordlessly and literally shot up off the floor. An inch shy of the ceiling, he slammed into an invisible barrier and fell. He got up and did it again, bouncing from ceiling to floor over and over, top to bottom, then left and right, bouncing like a little plastic ball back and forth, back and forth, back and forth, until finally he stopped bouncing and lay back in the middle of the circle, breathing heavily. Exhausted.

Reed stood. Ben saw the blue circle was complete.

"I bind you in the name of Hashtor and Emereth," Reed said. "I bind you in the pink, I bind you again in the blue, and for a second time in the name of Hashtor and Emereth, I bind you to answer true."

Diehl screamed.

"How did you first learn of the Q-Ray?"

"The Mad Thinker!" Diehl said. "In the strand that was, but is no more, and will never be again. The strand that we—"

"Silence," Reed said.

Ben and Reed and Yates all exchanged a quick look.

The Mad Thinker?

"After that accident with the androids," Yates said slowly. "When Max was in the press all the time . . . didn't they call him—"

"Yeah, but . . ." Ben shook his head. "That doesn't mean anything."

Had to be another costumed weirdo, a supervillain they hadn't heard of. It couldn't be Max.

"What do you intend to do with it? The Q-Ray?" Reed asked.

Diehl screamed and shook his head, so violently that Ben thought for a second it might come off. *Shades of* The Exorcist, he thought.

"You are bound," Reed said. "Answer the question. What do you intend to do with the Q-Ray?"

"Chaos!" Diehl screamed. "Catastrophe! Destruction!"

Diehl shook his head again, and the building, all at once, shook with it.

Ben stumbled and righted himself just before he fell.

"Careful," Reed snapped. "The chalk line."

"Yeah, yeah," he said, and stepped back a few paces. So did Yates.

The building was still rumbling.

"What the hell's going on?" Ben asked, though the second the words left his lips, he knew the answer.

Diehl was going on. Inside the pink circle, the air shimmered and sparkled with energy.

Diehl's eyes glittered.

His face stretched.

Ben's eyes widened. That was what had happened before, when he'd attacked the first time, and—

"Reed. Look at the guy's face."

"I see it. He can't escape. The circle contains him."

"Yeah, well, this building contains us, and if it falls down—"

"It's not going to fall down," Reed said, at which point the floor beneath them all suddenly rose up, and they—and the building—began to topple over slowly.

Yates slammed into Ben. Ben slammed into Reed.

His body bent to hold the three of them as they fell toward the wall, which was in the process of becoming the floor. Steel groaned. Plaster cracked, dust fell.

"The chalk line!" Reed shouted. "Don't hit the chalk line!"

Ben strained to hold Yates back. He heard Reed straining as well.

"I bind you to stop," Reed said. "In the name of Hashtor and Emereth, I bind you—"

Diehl just screamed. The man was stretching out like a rubber band, stretching like Reed, only in this case, obviously, the stretching hurt.

The building lurched, leaning farther to the side.

"I'm an idiot," Yates said, and burst into flame. Free of gravity. Free of Ben, who, free of the pressure, stumbled and slipped, causing Reed to stumble, too.

Reed cursed.

"The chalk!" he said, and smudged the line. An instant later, there was a scream and a sudden rush of air, and something flew past Ben, and suddenly . . .

He and Reed were standing straight up, and so was the building. Straight and true and entirely undamaged.

Yates hovered in the air at the far end of the room.

And Diehl was gone.

"Magic," Ben said. "I hate magic."

Yates flamed off and set down.

"That didn't go as planned," he said.

Reed shook his head and knelt down next to the broken chalk. "It shouldn't have been possible. The chalk would hold him, Stephen said. He shouldn't have been able to affect anything outside the circle."

"Maybe it wasn't him," Yates said, looking at Ben. "Maybe he had help."

"Yates, for God's sake, how many times we gotta go through this?" Ben shook his head. "Doom is over in Europe, Doom is—"

"Well, then, how did he do it?" Yates said. "How did he escape?"

"Magic," Ben said.

"Helpful answer."

"Tony." Reed said. "Ben's right. It can't be Doom."

"How do you know that?"

"For one thing, Doom is a little preoccupied right now."

"What do you mean?"

"Stephen is behind the Curtain," Reed said. "He's aiding certain resistance elements there."

"Resistance?" Ben didn't get it for a second. "Oh. Against Doom."

"Yes. Now, it may be possible that Diehl is receiving help from another outside source, I'll grant you that. We can check our instruments, see what sort of readings we got for these last few minutes, although . . ." Reed shook his head. "Eldritch energies tend to be nondirectional, so even if we have readings . . ."

"We can make a few informed guesses, though," Yates said. "Even in the absence of that kind of data. Diehl gave us some clues. The Mad Thinker, he said."

The room fell silent.

"Hey, come on," Ben said. "We don't seriously think he was talking about Max—do we?"

Yates sighed. "I don't know. Doesn't make sense to me, but . . ."

Both he and Ben turned to Reed, who waited another minute before replying.

"Some of the answers Diehl gave," Reed began, "lead me to think that almost anything is possible."

"No," Ben said. "Max couldn't have anything to do

with this. Diehl almost killed Max the first time he showed up. How could—"

"'Some of the answers Diehl gave,'" Yates interrupted. "Could you be a little more specific, Reed?"

Ben frowned. Some of the magician's words had, for some reason, rung a bell with him, too. "Strands, Diehl said. The strand that was. What the heck does that mean?"

"I'm not prepared to answer that at the moment," Reed said.

Yates threw up his hands in disgust.

"Thanks again for the helpful response."

"I'm sorry," Reed said. "That's the best I can do at the moment."

"Come on, Reed," Ben said. "You know something else, you gotta share it with us."

"I will. Soon. I promise. I just need to . . ."

Footsteps sounded. He looked up as Sue walked in the door.

". . . submit to an examination, I believe, which my personal physician is here to remind me . . ."

His voice trailed off.

Sue was crying.

"Johnny died," she said. "Johnny's dead."

11

AN HOUR LATER, THE THREE OF THEM—BEN, Yates, and Reed—were back in the command center. Sue was in Reed's quarters, waiting for him to return. Johnny's body was still up in medical.

"When the three of us are finished here," Reed said, "we're going to call her parents. Let them know. Make the funeral arrangements."

Ben sighed heavily. He couldn't believe this was happening. It all had an air of unreality to it.

He couldn't believe how upset he was. He hadn't seen Johnny in ten years, before this morning, and yet . . .

It felt, in some ways, as if he had lost a brother, too.

"Then Sue's leaving. Going to stay with a friend downtown," Reed said. "Because we have a lot to do. A lot to plan for."

"Diehl's coming back, you think?" Yates said.

Reed nodded. "It's a certainty. He wants the Q-Ray. He won't stop until he has it."

The far wall of the command center was taken up in its entirety by a multiuse, user-configurable display screen. Right now, it showed all the data they had related to Diehl's two appearances, a series of graphs and blinking lights and instrument readouts. Reed and Yates were sitting next to each other at the command console; Ben stood next to the display wall, studying the readouts, a lot of information that looked to him as if it could be summed up in a single simple phrase.

Diehl was getting stronger. Much, much stronger.

Ben shook his head. "We're gonna need more chalk."

Reed shook his head. "It won't work twice."

"Why?"

"It just . . . won't. Magic," Reed said.

"Same for the gloves, I assume?"

Reed nodded. "One of the reasons I prefer science to sorcery. Replicable results."

"You and me both, buddy."

"So what do we do?" Yates asked. "Diehl is as powerful as Doom ever was. Maybe more so."

"I agree," Reed said.

Ben took a deep breath. "It hurts me to say this, guys, but maybe . . . maybe we ought to call the Avengers."

"No," Reed said.

"Why not?"

"I need to talk to Stephen," Reed said. "He'll have advice. He'll want to hear about Agatha, anyway. Miss Harkness."

"That doesn't really answer my question," Ben said. "Why not call the Avengers? I mean, Thor, the guy's a god, right? If anybody can handle Diehl . . ."

Reed shook his head.

"I have an idea," Yates said. "Why don't we just destroy it? The Q-Ray."

"I'm with you there," Ben said.

Both men looked at Reed.

"I'm not prepared to do that at this time."

Yates slammed a fist down on the console. "I am getting sick and tired of you playing God, Reed. Why can't you just tell us what's going on?"

"There's a reason," Reed said. "You just have to trust me on this, Tony. Please."

"We have to trust you, but you can't trust us."

"That's not it," Reed said. "It's more a matter of burdening you with certain knowledge, which I don't feel . . ."

"Burden away," Yates said. "I can handle it."

"Me, too," Ben chimed in.

"No."

"So we just do what we're told and hope for the best?" Yates said.

"For tonight," Reed said. "Yes."

Yates drummed his fingers on the console for a second.

"The hell with you." He shoved his chair backward and stood. "Ten years, I've gone along with you bossing me around like I was your personal errand boy, Reed. No more."

He headed for the door.

"Tony!"

Reed's voice stopped him.

"I need you here."

"But you can't tell me why."

"Because we're a team," Reed said.

Tony snorted. "A team. Sure we are. We're all sorts of close."

He walked out.

"The Fantastic Three," Ben said. "Got a nice ring to it, don't you think?"

Reed said nothing.

"You know I'm with you," Ben said. "No matter what. But Yates, you gotta give him something, Reed. You gotta make him feel . . ."

"I've locked Max out of the system, Ben."

"What?"

"I've locked Max out. Of the system, of the building, until I can . . ." Reed sighed. "Until I can sort through all this."

Ben didn't know what to say for a minute.

He walked to the nearest chair and sat.

"You gotta be kiddin' me."

"I don't want to do it, believe me, but . . ."

"You believe Diehl."

"I don't know. But I have to . . . I have to err on the side of caution, Ben. You can see that, can't you?"

"I don't know. I got no freakin' idea what's going on here, remember?" He shook his head. It was all too much right then—Johnny, and Diehl, and exclusionary Hilbert spaces, and Reed not trusting him with the truth. And Max. Where the hell was Max?

The whole world has turned upside down, Ben thought. He needed a place where he could just sit still for a few minutes and not have to think. Someone to talk to.

Alicia.

"I'm going home," he said.

"I was hoping we could discuss strategy."

"What's there to discuss? When the time comes, you tell me what to do, I'll do it."

"You're not an errand boy, Ben."

"You don't gotta tell me that. You do gotta tell Yates—if you want his help."

Reed nodded. "You're right, of course."

"Of course I'm right. I'll see you tomorrow," he said, and turned to go—

—and almost walked right into Sue, standing in the doorway.

"Excuse me—I didn't mean to eavesdrop, I just . . ."

Her eyes were red from crying.

"You were going to rest," Reed said.

She shook her head. "Mom and Dad, Reed. I have to call them."

"All right. We can do that."

Ben put a hand on her shoulder. "You take it easy, Suzy—okay? Sleep if you can?"

She nodded.

Ben turned back to Reed. "And don't forget."

"What?"

"Talk to Yates, will you?"

Reed nodded.

"I'll remind him," Sue said.

She put an arm around Reed's waist and managed a smile.

Ben smiled, too. Reed and Sue together again, at least for the moment. It felt right. The way things ought to be.

"Hey," he said.

They turned as one.

"No civilians in the command center."

Reed glared; Sue glared, too.

"It's a joke," Ben said. "Can't anybody around here take a joke?"

Clouds were moving down the Hudson. Rain came with them. Ben thought he could beat the downpour across the river, but he was wrong. He was soaking wet by the time he got home.

Benjy and Tatianna were zoned out in front of the TV set.

"Hey," he said. "How was school?"

"Good," Tatianna said. "Except Jack Nelson threw a rock at me, so I threw one back, and then Mr. Wilkins yelled, and I got in trouble."

He patted her on the head. "Well, you know. Stuff happens. You gotta work it out."

She nodded absently.

"How about you, Benjy? What'd you do today?"

His son frowned. "Dad. You're blocking the TV."

"Right. Sorry." He watched his kids for a minute, just taking them in until he realized he was staring, and then he watched what they were watching for about as long as he could stand, which was on the order of ten seconds. Then he went into the kitchen.

Alicia was at the stove, pouring tea.

She turned at his approach, and her eyes widened.

"Ben?" She rushed to his side. "What happened to your hand?"

"Oh, that." He'd almost forgotten he was wearing a cast. "No big deal. A little break."

"A little break? Ben . . ."

"It's nothing, all right? I'm fine."

She frowned, and her eyes went right, in the direction of the kitchen table.

Ben turned. Rose was sitting there, dabbing at her eyes with a tissue.

"Rose," he said, and bit his tongue just in time to

stop from asking how she was, because it was clear from a single glance that she was not well.

"Hello, Benjamin," she said, and stood up—all five feet of her.

He crossed the room and gave her a hug.

She was crying when they broke the embrace.

"It's going to be all right," Ben said. "We're going to find Max, he's going to be fine, everything's going to be fine. I promise you."

"Max is downstairs, Ben," Alicia said.

"Oh."

Rose put a hand on his arm. "Will you talk to him, Benjamin? He's . . . I don't know what the matter is. He won't tell me anything."

Rose was the only person in the world—other than his grandma—who had ever called him Benjamin. It made it hard for him to refuse her anything.

"Sure," he said. "I'll go talk to him."

"Here." Alicia handed him a cup of tea. "Take this. Maybe it'll help him relax."

"Relax," Ben said. "Sounds like a good idea."

He turned and headed for the stairs.

Thunder crashed as Ben walked down to the basement. The storm was getting closer. The lights in Alicia's studio were on; the kids had been down there, it looked like to him, using one of the sketchpads that Alicia kept out for them. There were drawings of monsters, and bad guys, and good guys, too. Ben was pleased to see some pictures of the FF in there, though they'd mixed up the some of the heroes and villains, put the bad guys in some of the *4* uniforms.

Fantastic Four, Ben thought. He wondered if Yates was coming back. He wondered if Reed would remember to call him.

Most of all, he wondered what was going on with Max.

He pushed through the door into his workroom.

It was pitch black. No lights on.

"Max? You in here?"

No response.

"I got your tea."

Thunder sounded again. Lightning flashed, brightening the room for an instant.

Showing him Max, sitting on an overturned milk crate in the center of the room. Elbow on his knee, chin resting on hand. *He looks like the statue,* Ben thought. *The Thinker.*

The Mad Thinker.

Stop it, Ben told himself, and cleared his throat.

"All right. So I know you're upset about game nineteen. Tell you what I'm going to do. I'm gonna give you that move over. Seeing as how you never actually took your finger off your man. Although you never actually had your finger on the man in the first place, now, did you?"

Max said nothing.

"Okay. So it's not game nineteen, I'm guessing."

Ben waited.

And waited.

"Max . . ."

"A curious thing, Ben. My commlink is no longer active."

Ben sighed heavily. "Oh, boy," he said, because he couldn't think of anything else to say.

He brushed his hair back from his forehead, turned on his heel, and paced.

"A lot of crazy things happened today, Max. A lot of terrible things."

"Yes," Max said. "I'm aware."

"You're aware?"

"It's my system, Ben," he said, and there was a touch of anger in his voice. "I designed it, I implemented it. No one can lock me out. Not even Reed."

Thunder cracked again. Lightning flashed.

Ben turned in time to see Max's head come up, to catch a glimpse of his friend's face.

It was like looking at a stranger.

Max was as disheveled-looking as he'd been this afternoon—more so. His clothes, his hair, his expression . . .

His eyes.

The Mad Thinker, Ben thought again, and then the room went dark.

Ben didn't know what to say next.

"Though he may be right," Max said suddenly.

"Huh?"

"Reed. He may be right, you know. I may have told Diehl about the Q-Ray."

"What do you mean, you may have told him?"

"Just that," Max said. "It is possible. I really don't know. My head is full of possibilities at the moment."

"Max. You're freaking me out a little bit. How could you not remember something like that? You think Diehl did some kind of magic on you, tricked you into—"

"No, no, no," Max said. "Not at all like that."

"Then what?"

Max was silent a moment.

"I wouldn't want to burden you, Ben. Really, I wouldn't. You're much better off not knowing."

Reed saying those words had made him angry. Hearing them again, hearing them from Max . . .

A little chill went down Ben's spine.

"I'm sorry about Johnny, Ben. I know you were friends."

"Yeah. Thanks." Suddenly, it seemed stupid to be talking in the dark. "Let me turn on the lights here," he said, and before Max could object, he went to the wall and flipped the switch.

When he turned back, the stranger he'd glimpsed in the dark was gone, and it was just his friend sitting in the chair.

Ben had to smile.

"No offense, Max, but you've looked better."

Max smiled, too—for a second. Then the smile disappeared.

"I am sorry, Ben. For not being there today. I could've . . ."

"Forget that. What's done is done. Water under the bridge. But you gotta tell me what's going on, Max. What's wrong? Rose is up there, and . . ."

"I know," Max said, and got to his feet. "I know she's upset, I know you're upset, but really, Ben—I can't tell you. I won't tell you."

Ben frowned.

Now he was angry again.

"I am going to talk to Reed, though. Tonight," Max said hurriedly. "Then he and I—we'll need to decide what to do."

"Okay, but where were you today, Max? What were you doing?"

He managed a rueful smile. "What I do best. Thinking."

"About . . ."

"Different things." He shrugged. "Possibilities."

"Such as . . ."

Max was silent a minute.

"Where I would be—who I would be—if I hadn't met you, and Reed. If I wasn't part of the group . . ."

"You'd be locked in a lab somewhere, playing with rats and circuits. My guess."

Max didn't respond for a long minute.

"I hope so," he said. "God, I hope so."

It was the first time Ben had ever heard that particular word—God—escape his friend's lips.

Max sounded scared.

Alicia walked through the door.

"Dinner," she said.

"In a minute."

"Now, Ben. The kids are hungry."

"Now sounds wonderful," Max said. "Thank you, Alicia."

He walked past her and through the open door.

Ben stared after him and shook his head.

He wasn't done with this conversation yet.

"You come upstairs with that look on your face, you'll scare the kids," Alicia said.

"Sorry." His expression softened, and he smiled. "Rough day."

"I gather." She nodded at the cast. "You sure you're all right?"

"I'm sure. Sue looked at it."

"Sue?" Alicia frowned.

"Sue Storm."

"Sue was at the Baxter Building?" Alicia smiled. "Tell me she and Reed . . ."

"Maybe," Ben said. "I wouldn't be surprised."

"I never saw two people who belonged together more," she said. "Except us, of course."

"Right," Ben said. "Except us."

Arm in arm, they left the workroom. Alicia stopped at the bottom of the stairs.

"Those kids," she said, a trace of irritation in her voice. "I don't know how many times I've told them to clean up down here when they're finished."

She began picking up the drawings that Ben had seen before.

"Forgive me, Alicia," Max said from the top of the stairs. He hurried back down. "Those are mine, actually."

"Yours?" She frowned.

"Yes. Just some idle sketches. I'll take them," Max said, and bent to help her. He took the stack of paper she had in her hand. Ben caught sight of the drawing on top.

It had four people in Fantastic Four uniforms. There were Reed, and Yates—though the Torch looked different in some way that Ben couldn't quite put his finger on—and there was a woman with blond hair who looked an awful lot like Sue Storm.

And out in front of those three was a monster—a misshapen kind of humanoid, covered with what looked like orange rock.

Ben's breath caught in his throat.

"You have quite an imagination, Max," Alicia said, pointing at the creature. "Just what is that thing supposed to be?"

Max folded the drawing hurriedly in half, hiding it from view.

"Just doodling. While I waited for Ben."

He picked up the rest of his papers and went upstairs without looking back.

Alicia straightened and groaned.

"Yoga," she said. "This new class is killing me, Ben. I may need one of your world-famous massages tonight."

She smiled and looked at him, and the smile fell from her face.

"Honey," she said. "Are you all right?"

For a second, he couldn't answer. Literally couldn't get any words out of his mouth. He felt sick to his stomach, felt that same horrific sense of vertigo he'd felt yesterday when the kids had jumped on him, when he'd had to sit down in the middle of the floor to stop himself from throwing up. The thing in the picture . . .

"Fine," he managed. "I'm fine."

"You don't look fine. If I didn't know better, I'd say you were sick."

"I don't get sick."

"You don't break bones, either. But." She nodded toward the cast. "Seems like there's a first time for everything."

A buzzer went off upstairs.

"The potatoes," she said. "You coming?"

"Right behind you," he said, and turned for the stairs.

Max was looking down. For a second, their eyes met, and then his friend looked away.

And Ben stood by himself for a moment, in the basement of the house he'd lived in with his wife and children for the last five years, and felt completely, utterly, a stranger to himself.

He came upstairs and sat at the table, made all the motions of eating and drinking and polite conversation.

But he couldn't get the picture out of his mind.

He had to talk to Max about it, but Max wasn't talking. Max was clearly bothered as well, and where Ben at least went through the motions of normality, smiling at his kids, laughing at Alicia's attempts to lighten the mood, raving about the meal, Max ate quickly and quietly and didn't say a word.

He and Rose left before dessert.

The kids sensed his mood, somehow. They rushed through ice cream and headed upstairs without being prompted.

"Whatever's wrong with Max, he seems to have given it to you," Alicia said.

The two of them were at the sink; she was washing, he was drying.

"I guess," was all Ben could manage.

"You want to talk about it?"

He did. But he couldn't.

He didn't want to burden Alicia with his knowledge. His guesses. So instead he lied.

"Johnny was there today, too," he said.

"Johnny Storm?" Alicia smiled and shook her head. "My God. I haven't thought about him for years. What a cutie. He's married, isn't he? Divorced. Probably three times divorced. He's like Tony, women love him, he can't say no, he gets into trouble . . ."

She went on like that for another few seconds before Ben had to stop her and tell her the rest of what had happened today.

They left the rest of the pots and pans in the sink and went upstairs together.

After a while, Alicia fell asleep. Ben couldn't. He paced, and read, and roamed around upstairs till he woke up Benjy.

He sat with his son till the boy fell back asleep, and then he went downstairs and poured himself a drink and went into the living room to sit. The streetlights cast a pale yellow glow over his hand, and his glass, and the photo on the wall beside his chair—a blowup of the *Times* magazine cover, a posed publicity shot Yates had insisted the four of them take a few weeks after the accident.

They were all in their uniforms, dark blue back then, with simple black 4s in the middle of them. Reed and Max up front, sitting in chairs, he and Yates behind. Yates had flamed on one of his hands for show.

Ben was holding a bowling ball up with one pinkie. They were all smiling as if they owned the world, which, for a moment, they had. The headline read:

FANTASTIC FOUR: AMERICA'S
NEWEST HEROES

And in smaller type underneath:

THE HUMAN TORCH, THE THINKER,
MISTER FANTASTIC, MISTER INVULNERABLE

Mister Invulnerable. Ben hated that name, which put him in good company, as after a few weeks of being called Mister Fantastic, Reed had disavowed the title Yates's press team had come up with for him, too. Max had joined in, eventually, leaving Yates, as always, odd man out.

The names hadn't lasted, but their powers had. The group had.

Until today, Ben thought, taking a sip.

Today everything fell apart. Though really, now that he thought about it, everything had been falling apart for a while. Reed was always working in the lab, Yates was always preoccupied with his image, his companies, himself, and that left him and Max to do the work of the team, for the most part. And to play checkers.

And now Max was falling apart, too, which left

him. Mister Invulnerable. Not quite so invulnerable now, he thought, looking at the cast and thinking of the drawing.

He refilled his drink and sat in the living room, in the dark, until sleep took him.

He woke to the sound of a slamming door.

Ben opened his eyes. It was daylight.

He looked out the window in time to see Alicia and the kids hurrying off down the street, in the direction of school. For a second, he almost ran to catch them, then he saw the Roberta droid following and decided they were fine. He'd see them tonight.

He stood and stretched in the sun. Dave Dunton from next door jogged by and waved, and Ben waved back, and all at once, he felt a cloud lift. All that stress, Diehl and Johnny and Reed being mysteriously silent about everything, it had put him in a foul mood, a bad frame of mind. A paranoid frame of mind, he thought, where the sight of a simple drawing triggered all these crazy, ridiculous, stupid thoughts.

He was done with them, he decided. He was going to take today on its own terms, make a brand-new start.

He decided to work out. He put on an old Southside Johnny CD and some sweats, and went downstairs to the machines Yates's company had built for him. He worked till he was soaked through with sweat, then he showered and got dressed.

While he was putting on his shirt, the commlink sounded.

"Ben."

Reed was on the little screen, smiling, and Max stood behind him on one side, and Yates was on the other.

"Good news," Reed said. "I think we've found out how to handle Diehl."

"Working as a team," Yates said, putting a hand on Reed's shoulder. The two men smiled at each other.

"Hurry, Ben," Max said. "We need you here, too."

"I'm on my way," Ben said, and broke the circuit.

He was across the river in twenty minutes—his best time all month, another good omen.

On his way through the lobby, his stomach rumbled, and he decided to stop at Theo's for a little something else to eat.

He took a seat at the counter.

Olga had her back to him. She was making up a fresh pot of coffee.

"Two bagels when you get a chance," Ben said. "Toasted. Heavy on the cream cheese. Slice of onion, slice of tomato."

She turned around and screamed at the top of her lungs.

"Monster!" she yelled, and dropped the coffeepot. Glass shattered into a million pieces.

"Olga," Ben said, getting up from his seat. "What's the matter with you, what—"

"Monster!" she screamed again, and pointed right at him.

Theo came out from behind the counter with a knife.

"Monster," he said.

A rat scurried across the floor and stopped.

"Monster," it said.

Ben pushed himself back from the counter.

"What's the matter with all of you?" he said. "What are you—"

He stopped talking, because he'd caught sight of his hands, which were made of orange rock.

His arms, his legs, his chest were orange rock, too.

He was six feet tall, wearing blue underwear.

"The strand that was," the rat said. "The strand that will be again."

And then he screamed, too, and grabbed at his skin with one hand. He had only four fingers. He was a monster. He was the monster from Max's picture.

"Ben!"

He blinked and opened his eyes.

He was lying in bed. Alicia was propped up on one elbow next to him, her other hand on his shoulder.

"You all right?" she asked sleepily.

All he could do was nod.

She closed her hand on his, snuggled back onto her pillow, and was out again within seconds.

Ben lay awake for an hour—3:43 A.M. to 4:43

A.M.—before he decided he was not going to fall back asleep that night.

He gently pried his hand loose from Alicia's and got out of bed.

He changed and looked in on the kids—Benjy had his head buried under the blankets, Tatianna's bed was so full of stuffed animals she was practically falling off the edge. He moved his son, he moved his daughter's animals, and then he went down to the kitchen and started to write a note.

He got a page into it and realized that if Alicia read it, she'd think he was going off to kill himself. He ripped the paper up and started again. He made it much simpler this time:

Sleepyheads:
Had to go. Have a good day all, I'll see you tonight.
Love Ben (Dad)

He pinned it on the refrigerator and left the house.

Walking down the street, he had the urge to turn around several times, but he resisted.

He was afraid that if he looked back, the house would be gone.

12

"WHY SO EARLY THIS MORNING?" OLGA ASKED.

She was at the counter, pouring coffee in a to-go cup for him. He was getting those bagels from his dream, too, which he still hadn't been able to stop thinking about. They sat in a brown bag in front of him.

His right hand was in his lap, still in the cast, and his left—five pink-skinned fingers, no orange rock, completely and utterly normal, as was the rest of him—was *tap-tap-tap*ping silently on the Formica.

"One of those nights," Ben said. "Just couldn't sleep. Nightmares."

"Ah." Olga put the pot back on the burner and

the lid on his cup. "I dreamed, too. Terrible dreams. I was a girl, back in Kosovo, and the Gypsy King of the East was chasing me."

Gypsy King of the East, Ben thought. *Right.*

"Sorry, kid," he said, rising from his seat. "I don't have time this morning." Which was not the case at all, he had all the time in the world right now, but of all the things he did not want to talk about this morning, dreams were high on the list.

He gave Olga a five, told her to keep the change, and headed upstairs.

It wasn't even six yet—he was pretty sure Reed would still be asleep, which was fine with him, because he needed a little time by himself in the command center. He wanted to look up some of those things Reed and Max kept throwing out at him—Hilbert spaces, and strands, and the like—before he talked to Stretch. Before he thought about his dreams—and Max's drawings—again.

He walked into the command center, halfway through his first bagel, and stopped in his tracks.

Reed was there.

Max was there.

Yates was there, and so was Sitwell, and another man in dark sunglasses whom he didn't recognize, and so was Sue.

It was like his dream, except no one was smiling.

He chewed, swallowed, and spoke.

"What's up?"

"Something terrible has happened," Sue said.

Ben looked around the room.

Sitwell spoke. "At five-oh-two A.M. EST, we got an alert from one of our atmospheric satellites. Reading unusual weather patterns, virtually identical to the ones of March fourteenth."

"Unusual weather patterns," Ben repeated. "March fourteenth. Okay." He reached the console, put his bagel down, put the bag down, and took out his coffee. He took a big sip. "I'm listening."

"Reed and I were here," Max said. "When we got the alert, we had one of our sensor drones reposition to examine those disturbances."

Max and Reed were here, Ben thought. Working out whatever it was they needed to work out, which they'd obviously done, because . . .

"They turned out not to be weather-related at all," Max continued. "They were, in fact, energy surges, identical to the ones from March fourteenth."

"March fourteenth again," Ben said. "What does March fourteenth have to do with . . ."

His voice trailed off.

"March fourteenth," he said. "Elizabeth."

Max nodded. "That's right. We think it happened again."

"But . . . there hasn't been anything on the news, or—"

"It happened behind the Curtain this time,"

Sitwell said. "In Russia. Smolensk, to be more precise."

Ben took a second to absorb what he was hearing—and to remember what had happened.

March 14, Elizabeth, New Jersey. A crack in the sky. An energy vortex, of undetermined origin, that had come from nowhere and swallowed half a million people. It could have been a lot worse. Five miles to the north of its center was New York City; two miles south was Newark and the airport. If the vortex had hit there . . .

But that thought, no matter how many different ways Ben framed it, never went over with Reed. He was a glass-half-empty kind of guy.

He was thinking he should have stopped the vortex from hitting altogether.

The morning of the incident, Reed had come out of his lab, holding a printout and frowning.

"A lot of strange weather patterns," he'd said. "Been picking them up all week."

"Well—been a lot of strange weather all week," Ben had said, which was true enough, a lot of dark clouds over the city, but no rain, thunder and lightning but no big storms . . .

No big deal, they'd decided, and gone back to work.

An hour later, the vortex hit. Reed had gone right from the lab to the epicenter of the disturbance, without waiting for any of them.

He'd pulled a dozen people away from the edge of the phenomenon before collapsing himself. Ben, who was twenty minutes behind him thanks to a skirmish with a scrambled fighter jet out of a nearby Air Force base, had rushed his friend to Roosevelt, where Reed had stayed for the next twenty-three days, recovering from radiation sickness.

The dozen people he'd pulled out had been taken to Roosevelt, too—ten of them died.

Reed drifted in and out of consciousness for a week and a half, and when he finally woke up, the first thing he did was blame himself.

"I should have seen it coming," he'd said.

The signs were there, the clues were obvious, what sort of scientist was he that he couldn't piece it all together?

It was the same reaction he'd had after the accident—after the cosmic storms had hit their ship halfway between the moon and Mars. It was all his fault. He should have seen it coming. Which was nonsense, of course, but Reed wouldn't hear otherwise.

"Smolensk," Ben said. "Is that a big city, or . . . ?"

"Big enough," Sitwell said. "We've offered assistance, but no response yet."

"I hope you didn't mention our names," Ben said. "Doom would rather die than take help from us."

"Odds are, he's dead already," Sitwell said. "We have reason to believe he was near Smolensk."

"Oh?" Ben asked.

Jasper nodded. "According to Strange, at least."

"And what does Strange say now?"

"Nothing. We haven't heard from him since the last surge."

The whole room was silent a minute.

"So what's the next move?"

"We're trying to get one of the military satellites to reposition for a fly-by, so we can get surveillance, confirmation of the disaster. When that happens, we'll send a relief team in."

"Myself," Max said. "And perhaps one of the Avengers. We're trying to reach them now."

Ben looked at Max, then Reed, who had remained silent so far, and then finally Yates.

"Maybe I'm speaking out of turn here," he said slowly. "But—don't we have other fish to fry?"

"Actually . . ." Reed sat up straighter and cleared his throat. "I think it's the same fish."

Ben frowned. "Huh?"

Reed opened his mouth to speak again, and Sue put a hand on his shoulder.

"Let Max tell it, Reed. Please."

"Okay," Reed said, which was when Ben noticed his friend's voice sounded scratchy, a little weak. Reed didn't look too good, either, a little green around the gills. Sue was playing doctor, he realized; he guessed she'd examined him last night. He wondered what the results had been.

"I'll tell it," Yates said. "At least the parts I understand."

Ben frowned, suddenly—despite the circumstances—a little angry.

"Who all doesn't know about this?" he asked. "Just me?"

"We were here together," Max said, nodding to Reed. "Working it out, when the alert came in."

"I was sleeping," Yates said, pointing to the far end of the command center, in the direction of his quarters.

"Here?" Ben asked.

"Here." Yates nodded. "Having gone to Pennsylvania and gotten told to go to hell."

"I don't know about it." The man in sunglasses—the man to Sitwell's right, who Ben had assumed was some kind of security—spoke up. "If that makes you feel any better."

"It doesn't." Ben frowned again. "And who the heck are you, anyway?"

The man smiled. "If I told you," he said, "I'd have to kill you."

Nobody laughed.

"It's a joke," the man said. "Doesn't anyone around here have a sense of humor?"

Ben ignored him.

"Tell it, Max," he said. "Before I remind everybody about the rule again."

Max nodded. "Of course. I just want to say that

the comm had you coming this way, Ben, or we would have told you everything over the link."

"Okay," Ben said.

"Rule?" Sitwell asked. "What rule are you talking about?"

"Rule number one," Ben said.

Sue managed a smile. "No civilians in the command center," she said.

Reed smiled, too. So did Yates. Ben did as well, for a second.

Max wasn't smiling, though.

"It all goes back to the Q-Ray, Ben," he said.

"Why am I not surprised to hear that?" He looked at Reed. "So? Are we gonna destroy that thing or what?"

Max shook his head. "No. We can't."

"Why not? Didn't you just finish saying the Q-Ray was the problem?"

"It is."

"So . . ."

"The Q-Ray, however, is also the solution."

Ben frowned again. He could see this might take a while.

He sat down, opened the bag from Theo's, and took out the second bagel.

"Go ahead," he said. "Tell me."

The explanation started with Hilbert space. But it wasn't much of an explanation. Max was even worse than Reed at making complex concepts understandable. A few minutes in, the man in dark glasses—who turned out to be one of the president's national security advisers, a colonel named William Stryker—made his hands into a *T* shape and stood up.

"Time out," he said. "I don't know about you, Grimm, but I'm completely lost."

Ben nodded. "Yeah. Max, you better let Reed tell it."

"No." Yates exchanged a quick glance with Sue. "I'll do it."

Max shook his head. "What don't you understand? If it's a specific concept, I can—"

"Max," Ben said. "Buddy. Remember when you tried to help Tatianna build her volcano? Baking soda and vinegar?"

"Yes."

"She was up till, what? Nine o'clock? Nine-thirty? On a school night? Before you even started?"

"I thought it necessary to explain the basic concepts we were dealing with prior to commencement of the experiment."

"Yeah," Ben said. "Just let Tony do it, all right?"

Max frowned.

Yates took over.

"Forget the imaginary numbers, forget the alternate dimensions," he said. "Look at it like this. Hilbert space is a bubble, okay?"

Ben shrugged. "Yeah. Okay."

"In that bubble," Yates continued, "the normal rules of space-time do not apply."

Ben looked at Stryker. Both men nodded.

"Sure," Stryker said.

"Reed built the Q-Ray," Yates said, "to create a Hilbert space."

"You can move it up a notch, Tony," Ben said. "We don't need to spend the morning here."

"Just want to make sure it's clear," he said. "This is the important point. Under normal operating conditions, the Q-Ray can only create a finite Hilbert space. What we've recently discovered, though, is that the machine can be reprogrammed so that the space it creates is virtually infinite in size."

"Where does the exclusionary piece come in?" Ben asked.

Reed spoke up. "Once the space becomes infinite, it precludes the existence of any other spaces."

"Precludes?" Ben asked. "What's that mean, exactly?"

"Substitute *destroys,*" Yates said.

"Tony. *Destroys* is the wrong word," Max put in. "What happens at the mathematical level is—"

"Well, whatever word you want to use, it doesn't sound good," Stryker said.

"It's not," Yates said.

"Blow it up," Stryker said. "Blow this Q-Ray machine up, so your friend Dealey—"

"Diehl," Yates corrected.

"Diehl, excuse me," Stryker continued. "So that he can't use it."

"He already has," Yates said.

Stryker frowned. "Am I missing something?"

"A whole universe of somethings," Yates said.

"Elizabeth," Reed said.

Ben made the *T* sign. "Okay. I'm lost again."

The console chirped. Incoming communication from the security desk downstairs. On the monitor, Ben saw one of the O'Hoolihans and a woman he didn't know.

"That's my friend Millie," Sue said.

Reed nodded and told the android to send her up.

"I'll meet her in reception," Sue said, and put a hand on Reed's shoulder. "You take it easy, please. Doctor's orders."

He nodded. Sue said her goodbyes and left.

"Millie?" Ben said.

"She's going to help with the arrangements. For Johnny."

"Ah."

"Can we get back to the explanations, please?" Stryker asked. "Why can't we blow up the Q-Ray?"

"Because we need to use it."

"We need to use it." Stryker shook his head. "I'm lost again."

"Within the infinite, exclusionary Hilbert space the Q-Ray projects, what we believe occurs is the creation of a tabula rasa. Now the operator of the Q-Ray . . ." Yates continued.

"Wait, wait. The creation of a what?" Stryker asked.

"Tabula rasa," Ben said. "Blank slate."

Stryker looked at him funny. So did Yates.

"Hey," Ben said. "I took Latin."

He caught Reed's eye then, because the two of them had, in fact, taken Latin together, at ESU. The only class they'd ever been in at the same time. They shared a smile; a weak one, on Reed's part.

He didn't look good, Ben thought. *He didn't look good at all.*

"Exactly. A blank slate," Yates said. "Think of it as a void, within which the only living creature would be the operator of the Q-Ray."

"Then it's not actually a void, is it?" Sitwell said.

"No," Yates admitted. "Not exactly. Perhaps *void* is the wrong word. Forgive me. The point is, alongside the operator, there exist an infinite number of universes. Of possible realities," Yates said. "Have you heard of string theory?"

And Ben's heart began beating fast.

String theory, he thought. *Strands.*

"We think that the operator of the Q-Ray could stand within that void and play with the stuff of existence itself—all the possibilities that ever were—and pick and choose which ones would come into existence."

"The Mad Thinker," Ben said out loud. "In the strand that was."

Yates and Reed nodded.

Sitwell and Stryker both looked at him in confusion.

Max bowed his head and turned away.

"We think that this has happened already, that this universe we find ourselves in—"

"Wait a minute," Stryker said. "This universe?"

Ben felt sick to his stomach.

Benjy and Tatianna in his arms. The drawing. The dream.

"Possibilities," Max had said.

"Mr. Grimm?" Sitwell was looking at him and frowning. "Are you all right?"

"No," he said, and stood up. "I gotta get some air."

He walked out of the room before anyone could say a word to stop him.

He went to D level and took the access stairway to the roof.

He got to the edge and looked out across the river, toward Jersey. Last night's storm hadn't left the area; there were dark clouds over the Palisades and a light mist was in the air. People in the street below were carrying umbrellas—a sea of little red and black circles, moving up and down the sidewalks. He was reminded of those old Esther Williams movies, the swimmers and the formations they used to make, which made a design only when you looked down at them from above, as he was looking now.

Ben looked down and tried to find a pattern in the umbrellas. Part of him knew there would be none.

Part of him half expected them to form up into letters and spell out words. A single word, one he kept hearing in his head over and over.

MONSTER.

He heard a noise behind him and turned.

"Max."

"I came up to see if you wanted anything from the coffee shop downstairs. We're ordering breakfast."

"I ate."

"Yes, I know." Max smiled. "I thought you might want to eat again."

"Nah. Not hungry."

Ben turned around and faced the river again.

"That's not really why you came up," he said after a moment.

"No," Max agreed. "Not really."

"Diehl already used the Q-Ray," Ben said.

"We think so."

"We?"

"Reed and I. We had a long conversation about it, early this morning. We worked out the theory together. It explains Elizabeth, and Smolensk, and—"

"The drawing," Ben interrupted.

Max was silent a moment.

"The drawing was something I . . . dreamed. It may have nothing to do with . . ."

"I don't want to hear any more about it," Ben said firmly.

He looked out at Jersey again and pictured his house, his wife, and kids. They'd be up by now, Alicia making breakfast, packing lunches, going through the same school-morning routine that every family in the neighborhood went through, which was the only reservation she'd ever had about marrying Ben, or at least the only one she'd ever expressed to him.

"I want a normal life," she'd said. "I want to live in a neighborhood, not a fortress. I want to do my own grocery shopping, and my own cooking, and I don't want a bunch of men in dark suits and sunglasses following me everywhere I go."

"Guys in dark suits and sunglasses?" Ben had said, smiling. "Alicia, I'm not the president."

"No, you're not," she'd responded. "You're Mister Invulnerable."

Except that it was starting to seem like he wasn't. Not really.

"Okay," he said to Max. "How does it explain Elizabeth?"

"Elizabeth." Max nodded. "We—Reed and I—believe the energies released there to be the physical expression of an underlying, inherent tension brought into being simultaneously with the creation—or perhaps I should say re-creation—of the universe."

Ben leaned over the railing and laughed.

"What?" Max said.

He kept laughing, a lot longer than he needed to. All the tension that had been building up inside him these last few hours—the laughter was a way to let it go.

It was either that or break down and cry.

"I love you like a brother, buddy," he finally said, "but—"

"That wasn't clear—my explanation?"

"No," Ben said. "Not entirely. But I think I get the drift."

"An exploding volcano," Max said. "Like the one Tatianna built. It explodes because there is pressure building up beneath the surface. Lava, coming up from the mantle, seeking a way out through the earth's crust. It happens every day, an inevitable part of our planet's life cycle."

"Smolensk," Ben said. "That was another eruption—another expression of the underlying tension you were talking about."

"Exactly," Max said. "There will undoubtedly be more. Unless we remove the underlying source of tension."

"Which is what?" Ben asked.

Max made a weak attempt at smiling himself, then, and Ben, all at once, got it.

The problem was, he'd seen too many damn science-fiction movies. Alternate timelines, parallel universes, strands, whatever the hell terminology you wanted to use . . .

Things had to be set right, that was what Max was getting at. Set right, or they would get a whole lot worse.

He looked across the river again and said nothing for several long, long minutes.

13

EVENTUALLY, HE WENT BACK DOWN TO B LEVEL.

Everyone had moved from the command center to the staging area, where two tables had been set up. They were still waiting for breakfast to come from downstairs—not a surprise there, Ben thought, it was 8:40, and that was rush hour down at Theo's. Olga and Theo's kid and Theo himself straining to pour coffees and bag up danishes and doughnuts and bagels for the office workers, while still trying to get breakfast out to the tables for the tourists looking to get an early start on the day. It was a madhouse, no doubt. He wouldn't be surprised if their order didn't show for another half hour, at least.

Not that the time was going to waste.

Plans were being made.

Confirmation had come in on the Smolensk disaster; it looked worse than Elizabeth, Sitwell said. The good news was they'd gotten hold of the Avengers; Thor was coming. On his way, in fact, as were Hawkeye and the Wasp. Max had gotten the word and stayed up on D, waiting for them to show.

Ben wondered if Reed had somehow set that up. Arranged for the most powerful person on the planet to accompany Max, just in case . . .

Just in case what, he wasn't exactly sure. The Mad Thinker, in the strand that was.

Yates and Reed were talking about the Q-Ray. Sitwell was talking to Sue and her friend Millie, and Stryker was talking on the phone.

"Yes, sir," he said. "No, sir. I will make that very clear, Mister President. I will . . ."

In midsentence, Stryker abruptly stopped talking.

He dropped the phone and staggered.

Ben went to his side.

"Hey!" he said, putting a hand on the man to support him. "You all right, buddy?"

Stryker blinked. He looked momentarily disoriented.

Then he stood up straight and nodded.

"Fine," he said. "Thank you."

Ben picked up the man's phone, which had fallen to the floor, and handed it to him.

Stryker took it and hung up without saying another word.

Ben could've sworn he still heard talking coming from the receiver.

"Hey, Colonel," he said. "I think you just hung up on the commander-in-chief."

Stryker looked at him as if he had no idea what Ben was talking about.

"The president, I mean."

Stryker's eyes glinted with anger for a second. Then he smiled.

"My goodness," he said. "I believe you're right, Mister Grimm. I'll have to call back and apologize."

But instead of reaching for his phone, the man looked past Ben and toward the center of the room. His eyes settled on Reed and Yates, huddled together at one of the tables. He walked over to join them.

Ben, curious, followed a step behind.

"Excuse me. Doctor Richards?"

Reed looked up. "What is it, Colonel?"

"It's occurring to me," Stryker said, "that I should have a look at this machine of yours. The—what is it—Q-Ray?"

"Q-Ray, exactly," Reed said.

"Because having just spoken to the president about it and been unable to provide any detail whatsoever . . ."

"I'm surprised the president's interested in details," Yates said.

"Well." Stryker smiled. "He is the commander-in-chief."

"I'll brief him myself," Reed said. "Shortly. In the meantime . . ."

It was a cue for Stryker to leave. The man didn't take it.

"Of course, of course," Stryker said. "I understand. But considering how busy you are here, perhaps you'd allow me to lighten your burden, as it were. Take that task over for you. Mr. Grimm here," he said, nodding over his shoulder toward Ben, hanging a few feet back, who was surprised Stryker even knew he was there, "could show me the device."

"I don't even know where it is," Ben said.

"I'm the only one who does," Reed said, "and right now, I don't have time to give you a tour. I'm sorry, Colonel."

Stryker frowned. Ben saw the man's shoulders tense. He was getting angry and trying hard not to show it.

"I could order you," the colonel said. "On the president's behalf."

"You could," Reed said. "But I don't take orders from the president."

A vein in Stryker's forehead throbbed.

Blood trickled from the corner of the man's mouth.

"Hey," Ben said, stepping forward, "Colonel . . ."

"Don't touch my person!" Stryker yelled.

Ben looked at Reed, and then Yates, and then shook

his head. Who'd talk like that—"Don't touch my person"?

"I'm not gonna touch you, but . . . your mouth," Ben said. "You're bleeding."

Stryker reached up and touched his face. His fingertips came away red.

"Sit down, Colonel. Please," Reed said. "Sue is a doctor, she's in the next room. Ben, if you could ask her to come in here?"

"On my way," Ben said, turning for the door.

He took one step, and Stryker collapsed.

Sue was there a minute later, kneeling down next to the colonel. She had one hand on his neck and another on his wrist and was shaking her head.

"He's dead," she said.

"What?" Ben was stunned.

"My guess is a stroke of some kind—brain hemorrhage, possibly, given the bleeding. I can't know for sure without an examination."

"This is nuts," Ben said.

Sue stood up. "You say he had an episode just prior to this one?"

"Yeah, I think so. Looked like he almost fainted, but then . . . he seemed okay."

"Sounds exactly like a stroke."

"Excuse me a moment." Sitwell flipped his phone open with a little beep. "I need to make a call."

He walked to the far end of the room and started talking.

"Reed?" Sue asked. "How are you holding up?"

"I'm fine," he said.

"You're going to let Tony handle the machine, though? As we talked about?"

"Yes," Reed said. "I am."

"Handle the machine?" Ben frowned. "Somebody want to let me in on the plan here?"

"I'm going to operate the Q-Ray," Yates said. "When the time comes."

"And when exactly does the time come?" Ben asked.

"As soon as my lesson in higher-order imaginary spaces is finished," Yates said, smiling. "Could be another month at this rate."

"You're doing fine," Reed said. "These are complex concepts. Especially since I can't be entirely sure how the equations will translate to the physical reality you'll be experiencing within the Hilbert space."

"I'm glad you all know what you're talking about." That was Sue's friend Millie, who'd come in as well. Her face, all at once, looked familiar to Ben, though he couldn't quite puzzle out why.

"Yeah," Ben said. "I know the feeling."

He tried to smile then, to make light of it, as if it were a joke that the two of them shared. He and Millie, the stupid ones in the room, trying hard to keep up with the geniuses.

But, in fact, Ben knew exactly what Yates and Reed were talking about. What Yates was going to be doing.

He was going to turn on the Q-Ray, create this exclusionary Hilbert space, which would annihilate the entire universe, and then—

He would build it all over again.

The Mad Thinker and the strand that was.

A monster, made of orange rock.

His wife. His kids.

And suddenly, Ben didn't want to play stupid anymore.

"Here's the thing, though, Reed. How do you know what to destroy and what to save? What belongs and what doesn't? I mean, you're playing freaking God here, and how do you know if what you're doing is right?"

Everyone in the room fell silent.

Ben realized then he'd been shouting.

"Dammit," he said, and turned away.

Reed, finally, broke the silence.

"It's in the equations, Ben. At least, we think it is, Max and I. We think—"

"Did someone call me?"

Ben turned and saw Max enter from the command center.

"Not exactly," Reed said "I was just telling Ben about what we expect Tony to see within the Hilbert space. How he'll know what to do in there."

"I see."

Ben turned and looked at Max. If anyone understood his concerns, it would be him.

His friend's eyes, though, were strangely blank.

"Hey," Yates said. "Aren't you supposed to be in Europe? With the Avengers?"

Max nodded. "That's correct. However, I lost contact with their ship just a moment ago."

"Lost contact?" Ben said. "How?"

"Unclear. One moment the signal was quite strong, the next it had disappeared."

"That's weird."

"Exactly. That is why I was in the command center. Performing a diagnostic subroutine. If you'll excuse me, I'll—"

"Hang on a minute, Max," Reed said. "Maybe you can help me make this clear for Ben. To answer your question from before, Tony—or, rather, Tony's consciousness, we don't know if a physical form will actually survive the transition, or even have consciousness of its physicality—will find itself within a void, infinite in size."

"With the strands. You said all this already. My question is, how do we know which is the right strand—the right universe?"

Reed frowned. "I'm not making this clear. There is only one universe. It can take multiple forms. The one we want is, as described by the equations, simply the most likely one of all."

"You're right," Ben said. "You're not making this clear."

All at once, another question occurred to him as well.

"Diehl," he said. "Why is he coming after the Q-Ray now? What does he want to do with it?"

"We're not certain. He may simply want to continue experimenting with reality. He may—"

"Well, then, why didn't he just take it with him? After he used it?"

Reed frowned and thought a moment.

"That's a good question," he said. "I don't exactly know how to answer it."

"Sheesh," Ben said. "Gotta lotta holes in this theory of yours, Reed."

"Excuse me. Dr. Richards?"

Sitwell walked over, holding out his phone. "It's Colonel Fury, sir. He'd like to speak with you."

"Of course." Reed took the phone. "Nick?"

He listened a second and frowned.

"I don't know," Reed said. And then: "No. Nick, I'm sorry. I appreciate your intentions, but . . .

"Colonel Fury." Reed's voice had taken on an edge that Ben almost never heard. "I don't take orders from you."

He hung up the phone and handed it back to Sitwell.

"Problem?" Ben asked.

"He wanted me to show you the Q-Ray," Reed said to Sitwell.

Sitwell nodded. "Yes, I know. Halfway through our

conversation, the idea seemed to take hold of him. He thought it important."

Reed frowned again.

Before he could answer, Sue spoke up.

"We should move Colonel Stryker upstairs to your medical lab," she said, nodding to the body on the floor. "That way, when the funeral home comes . . ."

She was looking to Reed for an answer, but he was still frowning, still deep in thought about something.

"Sure," Ben said. "I'll do it."

He bent down to pick up the corpse.

"Ow," Yates said.

Ben straightened and looked at the man, who for a second had the oddest expression on his face.

"You all right?" Ben asked.

The expression cleared, and Yates smiled.

"Sure," he said. "Fine. You know, Reed, I was just thinking."

Reed looked up.

"Maybe," Yates continued, "maybe I should try a little hands-on with the machine—the Q-Ray. Do that while we discuss the theory. What do you think?"

Reed scowled.

"I think I'm getting very tired of people asking me . . ."

He stopped in mid sentence, looked at Yates, and then quickly looked away.

Something weird is going on here, Ben thought.

Reed cleared his throat.

"You know, Tony, maybe that's not such a bad idea," he said. "Give me a minute with Sue here, and then I'll take you down to it."

"Down to it," Yates said, and smiled. "Of course. Excellent."

"Ben," Reed said, nodding toward Stryker's body. "If you wouldn't mind . . . you could bring that and then meet us in medical. Max, maybe you can help him."

"I don't really need help, Reed," Ben said, and bent down again, and lifted the colonel's body.

"Come anyway, Max," Reed said. "You can help me with the machine."

Reed took Sue's hand as they started for the door. He whispered something to her; she looked confused.

Ben, a step behind with Stryker, caught a glimpse of his friend's face. Reed looked nervous. Reed looked scared.

Definitely something going on here, Ben thought.

"Richards," Yates called out.

Richards? Ben thought. Since when did Yates called Reed "Richards"?

"Be right back, Tony," Reed said. "Then we'll take a look at the machine."

"I don't think so," Yates said.

Millie suddenly darted in front of them, blocking the door.

"Millie?" Sue said. "What are you doing?"

Millie smiled. She had incredibly white teeth.

Seeing those teeth, seeing her smile like that, Ben suddenly remembered her name, realized why her face looked so familiar. Millie Collins. She was a model, or, rather, used to be a model, maybe ten, fifteen years back. TV, fashion shows, *Sports Illustrated* swimsuit issue, the works . . .

"Reed, Reed, Reed," she said. "You've figured it out. Haven't you?"

"Millie?" Sue said again.

"No," Reed said. "Not Millie."

And suddenly, Ben figured it out, too.

"Diehl," he said.

Millie laughed.

A little beep sounded. Ben turned and saw Sitwell had his phone out again and was starting to dial.

"No," Yates said. "I don't think so."

Sitwell looked up.

"Let's see," Yates said. "How does it work . . ."

He looked down at his hands, which, all at once, caught fire.

"Ah," he said.

His entire body burst into flame.

He raised his arms then, pointed them at Sitwell, and a jet of fire shot across the room and incinerated the S.H.I.E.L.D. agent where he stood.

"Oh, this is good," Yates said, looking down at his hands, which were still on fire. "This is excellent."

"Oh, my God," Sue said.

"Diehl," Ben said. "You son of a . . ."

Yates started laughing, too. "Diehl," he said, and shook his head. "Diehl."

"Reed?" Sue asked. "What's happening?"

"Doomsday," Millie said, stepping forward. "Chaos. Apocalypse. Armageddon."

She was still smiling. It was not a happy smile. It was a spooky, ghoulish, scary smile.

Reed began backing away from her, pulling Sue with him.

Ben set down Stryker's corpse and began backing away, too.

Those were the same words Desmond had used. And Diablo. So what had happened at Building Twelve . . .

That was part of this, too, connected in a way he couldn't quite figure out. Part of Diehl's plan, though how it all tied in—

"Ben," Reed said. "Max. You can't let him have the Q-Ray. Kill me if you have to, but don't let me tell him where it is."

"Not much chance of that," Ben said. "Especially since I don't have a freaking clue myself."

"You'll figure it out. The two of you," Reed said. "You'll figure it out. So promise me."

"I promise," Max said. The three of them had formed up into a circle, with Sue inside.

"Yeah," Ben said. "Sure. I promise. But if we can figure it out, what makes you think Diehl can't, too?"

"Diehl." Stryker's corpse sat up and started to laugh. "You keep saying Diehl. But Diehl's dead."

Ben looked around the room. Yates was still smiling. Millie was, too. And Stryker as well.

"Somebody let me in on the joke," Ben said.

The air in the center of the room began to shimmer. A form to take shape.

And Ben suddenly got it.

"I'm an idiot," he said.

Reed nodded. "We're all idiots. Every one of us."

"Not all of us," Ben said, realizing that if they got out of this, he was going to owe Yates a very big apology indeed.

Max said nothing.

"What do you mean?" Sue asked. "What's happening?"

"Like your friend said, Suzy. Armageddon. Apocalypse." Ben glanced toward the middle of the room, where the figure had just finished materializing.

A man in a green cloak.

A man in a metal mask.

Not Jembay Diehl at all.

"Doomsday," Ben finished.

"Victor," Reed said.

Doctor Doom, energy crackling around his form, turned to face them.

14

THE GREEN CLOAK SWIRLED.

The building itself rumbled and shook.

Six inches off the ground, arms folded across his chest, Doom hovered in midair and spoke.

"Where is it, Richards?" he said. "Where is the machine?"

Reed didn't answer.

Doom. Of course it was Doom. Doom controlling Stryker, Doom controlling Sue's friend, Doom controlling Yates, and Diehl, and—

"It was you," Ben said. "You're the one who used the Q-Ray. Not Diehl. You . . ."

"It was neither of us, if you want the precise truth. It was him." Doom pointed at Max.

The Mad Thinker, Ben thought.

His friend's eyes remained strangely blank.

"It took me time to discover that reality had been warped; time to discover how, and who had done it. Diehl was the key; he had been my pawn, once. His mind remained tied to mine. I used that link to . . ."

Sue stepped forward. "You're responsible for Johnny's death."

"I'm responsible for nothing." Doom raised a gloved hand and pointed a finger at Ben. "Yet."

There was something weird about the bend of his finger, the shape of the glove, as if there wasn't a hand underneath it at all. *There is something different about Doom himself, too,* Ben thought. Not just the hands, he seemed bigger, more powerful, he seemed . . .

His legs ended in hooves.

Ben looked up and found Doom's eyes on his.

"I have congressed with certain powers," he said. "I have made deals, paid certain prices, but that is not your concern, Grimm. Your concern, here and now, is seeing that I get what I want, so that you get a few more moments of life. You and your friends. Your wife. Your children."

Ben stepped forward, in front of Reed and Sue and Max. "Leave my family out of this."

"I have little interest in your illusory family," Doom said. "What I want is the Q-Ray."

Illusory family. Ben resisted the urge to turn around and look at Reed.

Doom seemed to know as much about what was going on here as they did.

"I know more," Doom said. "Much, much more."

For a second, Ben didn't answer.

Doom was reading his mind, was all he could think.

How was Doom reading his mind? He didn't have that kind of power. He . . .

"I have it now," Doom said.

"Yeah," Ben said. "I guess you do."

"Victor." Reed spoke for the first time. "What have you done to yourself?"

"I have followed the path toward truth," Doom said. Ben could hear the smile in his voice, saw it, in his mind at least, on his face, Doom's once-handsome face, scarred in the laboratory accident that had gotten him expelled from ESU. "The same path that took you to Mars, to the cosmic storms, I have followed to my own destiny."

"If you know as much as you say you do," Reed replied, "you know that the energies you're talking about are too powerful to be harnessed."

"Harnessing those energies is not my intent."

Ben frowned. "I don't get it."

"Of course you don't. Pink skin or orange rock, you're an idiot, Grimm. Now, let's see if you know anything that concerns me."

All of a sudden, a knife cut into the top of Ben's brain, and he dropped to his knees and screamed.

Doom was in his mind, he realized. Doom was . . .

Images flashed past. The Q-Ray, himself, Alicia, Johnny, Max, the ship, the cosmic storm, the radiation pounding him like bullets, the heaviness in his arms, his legs, the alarm on the ship, sounding again and again and again, him screaming . . .

He was screaming now, Ben realized. He was rolling on the floor like a baby and screaming.

The pain stopped. Ben opened his eyes. He was lying on his back in the middle of the floor, halfway across the room from where he'd been. His throat was raw.

"Grimm doesn't know," Doom said. "Mister Yates?"

"Stop it," Reed said, and got to his feet. "I'm the only one who knows. I'm—"

Yates screamed out loud and put both hands atop his head.

He dropped to the floor as if he'd been poleaxed. He shuddered once and lay still.

"Nor Yates," was all Doom said then, and he turned his attention to Max.

He frowned for a second.

And then blue fire shot from his hands, and Max burst into flame.

"MAX!" Ben screamed.

Circuitry sparked. Rubber burned.

It wasn't Max. It was an android, a duplicate. So where was . . .

"Good Lord," Reed said, and turned several shades paler. "Max."

Doom spun slowly in midair, concentrating.

"Wherever your friend is, he's not in the building," Doom said at last. "So. That leaves you, Richards. And I hesitate to trespass in your mind. I worry about breaking things I may need later. But . . ."

He motioned with one glove, and Sue, who had been standing behind Reed, was suddenly standing in front of him.

"Perhaps there is another way to obtain the knowledge I seek."

"Leave her alone," Reed snapped.

"Tell me where the machine is."

Reed said nothing for a long moment.

"We were friends, Victor," Reed said. "Don't you remember?"

Ben remembered; they'd been at ESU together, the three of them. Reed was supposed to be Doom's roommate—Victor von Doom, Ben had heard the girls in the sorority next door talking about him as he walked into the dorm that first day. Victor von Doom. European royalty, right at their school. Handsome, they said. Dark. Mysterious.

And totally nuts, as Ben and Reed found out that first semester, when Doom had blown up half the dorm in a futile attempt to breach the wall between this world and the next, between the realm of flesh and that of spirit, to combine the powers of science and sorcery and—

"Friends." Doom shook his head. "The blood of kings flows in my veins, Richards. My ancestors were of the Order of the Dragon. I can name them through sixteen generations, six hundred years. You are a peasant, descended from peasants. Friendship between the two of us is as unlikely as—"

Ben screamed his best kamikaze war yell and charged.

Doom flicked a wrist, and Ben went flying backward, through the wall, and out into the visitor reception area.

He slammed into the wall and slumped to the floor.

He sat there a minute, sat there until he realized he was lying in something wet. Brown liquid, a puddle of it. Coffee—there was a tray of overturned cups on the floor. Two big white plastic bags of food as well.

"The Gypsy King," someone whispered.

Ben looked up and saw, not five feet away from him, Olga, back pressed against the wall, trembling like a leaf. Beyond her, he saw a stretcher, with a black body bag lying on top of it. Johnny. Prepped and ready to go to the funeral home.

"My dream," she whispered. "The Gypsy King of the East."

"Get out of here," Ben said, getting to his feet.

"The Gypsy King," Olga said again.

"The elevator," Ben said. "Go."

And then he went himself, charging back through the hole in the wall he'd made, hoping that Olga would do as he told her, but not having time to take her by the hand and guide her himself. Poor kid. She was scared to death.

He oughtta be scared, too, Ben knew, but he just didn't have time.

Then he burst into the staging area again, and suddenly he *was* scared.

Doom was holding Thor's hammer.

That wasn't right.

For one thing, nobody but Thor could hold Thor's hammer. That was one of the rules, Ben knew that.

For another . . .

If Doom was holding the hammer, where was Thor?

And where was Sue's friend, and Yates's body, and Stryker, and—

The wall. The far wall was gone, just gone, Ben was looking out into the sky, and open space, and the city beyond, and that wasn't right, because, among other things, that was a load-bearing wall. Ben knew that from the plans he and Reed had drawn up way back when. And if that was a load-bearing wall, then the two floors above them should have collapsed by now, and . . .

Magic. He hated magic.

Ben tried to gather his thoughts. Reed and Sue were huddled together in the center of the room, their backs to the open sky. Doom hovered above them.

". . . and there is a strand, Susan, where we are married."

Sue, tears streaming down her face, suddenly stood up. Awkwardly, stiffly, as if she were being forced.

"You killed her," she said. "You killed Millie, and she never did anything to you. She . . ."

"And there is a strand," Doom continued, paying no attention to her whatsoever, "where Richards and I are business partners, where the three of us are close, close friends, brothers and sisters in all we do. A strand where this"—he held out the hammer—"has the power to hurt me. Not here, though. Not now. Not the hammer—"

It disappeared.

"Or the one who wielded it, or any creature born of man and woman."

"You're a monster," Sue said.

Reed stepped forward. "Victor. I don't know what it is that you intend to accomplish, but I—"

"Chaos," Doom said. "Apocalypse. Armageddon. Now, where is it?"

Reed took Sue's hand and put her behind him.

"Never."

"I will take her," Doom said. "And then—"

Ben charged.

Doom, without turning, held up a hand, and Ben

ran smack into something, a force shield of some kind, and flew backward.

"—I will march with her, along the path I have walked, two months through the underworld, to the mountains of madness, past the nine white dogs, past horrors unimaginable, horrors that will shred all remnants of sanity, horrors that will ensure . . ."

"Stop it," Reed said.

Ben was about to charge Doom again when he realized how stupid and futile that effort would be.

What could he do? *Think, Ben, think.*

The door to the command center was directly opposite him. If he could get there, he could—what? Call the Avengers? Call S.H.I.E.L.D.? Fat lotta good that would do.

He could, Ben reflected, call Alicia and say goodbye.

"Ben." He looked up.

Max stood between him and Doom. He smiled and flickered. Not Max. A hologram.

"The core, Ben," he said, and disappeared.

Doom turned toward where the hologram had been, and the wall behind him exploded.

Androids charged into the room.

O'Hoolihans, and Robertas, and more Maxes. A Reed. A Mister Invulnerable—him—dressed in one of those red uniforms the team had worn for about a week, which made Ben frown. When the heck had Max built one of him, and where was the real Max, anyway?

"Futile," Doom said, and raised a hand, and out of

the dozen or so that had entered, more than half were suddenly just gone.

Which was when a beam of red light shot out from the opposite direction entirely and hit Doom square in the chest.

He flew backward out of the building and into the empty space beyond.

Two more Maxes, each holding an energy blaster, stepped into the room.

"Nice shooting," Ben said, and smiled for a second.

He looked at Reed and at Sue, who had collapsed on the floor again.

Reed turned and looked at him, too, and Reed wasn't smiling.

"Now, Ben," Reed said, looking right at him. "You have to do it now—while you can."

For a second, Ben didn't know what he meant.

"Oh, no," he said then, getting it. "I am not going to . . ."

"If you don't kill me," Reed said, "everyone dies. All of us. Elizabeth a million times over."

"We'll find a way to stop him," Ben said. "Strange. Doctor Strange. If Doom survived, then maybe he did, too. Maybe—"

"Stephen's dead, Ben. Doom killed him. He killed him, and Thor, and the other Avengers, too. He's changed—Victor. Something's happened to him, he—"

"The feet," Ben said. "Yeah, I saw. Come on. Explanations later. For now . . ."

The two androids exploded.

Ben looked to the sky and saw a green dot, growing larger.

He grabbed Sue's hand and helped her to her feet. "The core. Max said . . ."

The door to the core, and the inner stairwell, exploded.

"Okay. Not the core."

Ben changed directions and dragged Sue, Reed a step behind, into the reception area.

Olga was exactly where he'd left her, her back pressed to the wall, right next to the elevator. She stared over Ben's shoulder, her face wide with terror.

"Hit the call button," Ben said, knowing it was no escape route, but looking for a few seconds, that was all, something to buy time while he—or Reed—or somebody—came up with a plan, something.

Olga didn't move.

Ben reached for the button, and suddenly, it was gone.

"Enough," he heard a voice say, and turned.

Doom, a gaping hole in his chest, a hole through which Ben could see nothing but blackness and fire . . . What had happened to Doom's body, what was that blackness? How in the world was it possible that Doom was still on his feet? Well, not really on his feet, he was floating in midair, but why wasn't he dead, what he, in fact, was—

"The Gypsy King of the East," Olga said again, her voice barely a whisper.

"You got that right," Ben said, bracing himself for an attack.

Doom suddenly froze in midmotion.

He was staring, Ben realized. Not at him, but—

Olga.

"*K'ol Byola,*" Doom said, or words like that, words he spoke in a thick, rough Eastern European accent.

Ben risked a glance behind him.

Olga's right hand was on the necklace she wore, a necklace of colored beads and coral, with a disk of dull copper metal at the end of it.

"Where did you get that?" Doom demanded, advancing.

Olga was holding tight to the necklace around her neck, mumbling something that Ben thought, for a second, was nonsense, until he realized it was another language altogether.

"I asked you a question, child. Where did you get that?"

"Grandma Irina," Olga said, putting her right hand on the necklace. "Give me strength. Give me power. Protect me, Grandma Irina, please."

Doom had stopped moving.

"Irina?" he said, his voice barely above a whisper. "The gypsy, Irina? Mircea's gypsy?"

Olga squeezed her eyes shut. "Protect me from the evil in the East, from the Beng who wanders this world and the underworld, protect me—"

"Yes," Doom said, more to himself than anything

else. "No wonder it wasn't at the Embassy. The gypsy, she kept it with her, the whole time she kept it with her."

"I call upon the power of *K'ol Byola*—the power of the circle. The power of life itself," Olga said, and the necklace—and then Olga, and then the air around her—began to glow, a faint orange color that grew outward in a circle, till it became a dome. A bubble, enclosing them. Keeping out Doom.

Hilbert space, Ben thought for some reason.

The bubble began to grow.

15

OF ALL THE CRAZY THINGS THAT HAD HAPPENED over the last few days . . .

This, by far, was the craziest.

Ben looked back at Olga, who wore an expression somewhere between terror and exhilaration.

"I remember now," she said. "At the camp in Kosovo. The soldiers. The bullets . . . It was real. It was all real."

Her hand on the necklace was glowing bright orange now, lit as if from within.

Kosovo. Ben knew she'd been in the camps; but as far as what she was talking about now, he had no idea. And how she was doing what she was doing . . .

"Remind me to give you a bigger tip next time," he said.

There was a sudden, deep rumble—like thunder in the distance.

Ben looked up and saw Doom outside the bubble, visible as if through a stained-glass window. He hit the bubble, with his fists first, and then with an energy blast of some kind that came from his fingers.

The bubble shook; the surface rippled, like waves passing on the ocean.

"The amulet is mine," Ben heard Doom say, his voice muffled by the barrier between them, as he moved around it, a shadowy figure seeking a way in. "From my ancestors, through Tepes himself and Mihnea and then Voica, from Mircea before it was stolen, it is rightfully mine, and . . ."

He moved on, to the other side of the bubble, and his voice faded away.

"I call upon the power of the circle," Olga chanted. "I call upon the power of life itself."

"Ben." Reed appeared at his shoulder. "Who is this woman?"

"Who is she?" A year, at least, Olga had been working right downstairs, and Reed didn't know who she was? "This is Olga. She works at Theo's," he said. "Among other things, obviously."

Reed walked around in front of her.

"The runes on the necklace," he said, leaning over.

"They look like the ones on those gloves Stephen gave us."

He reached out a hand.

Sue intercepted it.

"I think," she said, "we ought to let her concentrate."

"Right," Reed said. "Of course."

"What we ought to do," Ben said, "is come up with a plan. A way to stop Doom from getting to the machine."

"Doom and Max," Reed said.

Ben frowned. "Huh?"

"It was an android. He fooled me. He went . . ." Reed looked up at Ben. "We need a plan. We have to get to the machine, right now."

"Wait, wait, wait," Ben said. "What's this about Max? What do you mean, he fooled you?"

Before Reed could answer, there was a sound like a roaring wind, and suddenly there was a tear in the bubble.

A gloved hand reached through.

Ben turned back to Olga.

Her eyes were closed, her brow beaded with sweat.

"I call upon the power of the circle," she was still saying. "I call upon the power of life itself."

"Hang in there, kid," Ben told her, the words sounding stupid even as he said them. He went to pat her on the shoulder, then thought better of it. Sue was right; distracting her this second would not be a good idea.

"No time for a plan," Reed said. "Ben. Kill me."

"Will you stop that, already?" Ben snapped. "If I kill you, who's going to teach me how to work the Q-Ray?"

Reed had no answer to that.

"Exactly," Ben said.

The glove on Doom's hand fell off.

Underneath it was a claw of some kind.

"Oh, my God," Sue said.

"From what he was saying before, I gather he's mated with some kind of demon," Reed put in, in a very matter-of-fact voice.

"The power of the circle," Olga said in English, and there was a note of desperation in her voice now. "The power of life itself. The power of the circle. The power of life itself."

The claw seized hold of the edge of the bubble and tore at it.

Olga gasped and muttered something in what sounded like that same harsh, guttural language that Doom had used.

The bubble wavered.

She kept chanting, her voice ragged, not much more than a whisper.

Right then, Ben remembered something else Strange had told him about sorcery.

It was about willpower, about belief—and not just on the part of the magician.

He took Olga's hand in his good one.

"The power of the circle," he said, right along with her. "The power of life itself."

She looked up, startled for a second, and then managed a smile.

"Ben," Reed said. "We need to focus on the task at hand."

He was about to argue with Reed, but Sue stepped forward.

"It seems to me that's what they're doing," she said, and took Olga's other hand.

"The power of the circle," the three of them said together. "The power of life itself."

The amulet began glowing brighter again. Sue and Ben exchanged a quick glance. Whatever they were doing, it was working.

"Reed!" Sue said, and motioned to him with her free hand.

He looked at her dubiously.

"Reed!" she said again, more urgently, and he—with a reluctant shrug—joined hands, first with her, then with Ben, putting his free hand on Ben's cast.

"The power of the circle. The power of life itself."

"If Max has reached the machine," Reed said to Ben, under his breath, "then—"

"The power of the circle," Sue said loudly, glaring at Reed. "The power of life itself."

He nodded and went back to chanting. For a minute.

"We can't keep this up forever," he whispered out

of the side of his mouth. "Doom will find a way to get through this, and then—"

"One thing at a time, Stretch," Ben said, and then resumed the chant. The power of the circle. The power . . .

A second later, he heard Reed chanting right along with him. The same phrase, over and over again. A mantra—like at Alicia's yoga class. He'd gone and watched once, stood in the little waiting area while she finished the exercises, or positions, whatever it was they called them, sat there with her legs crossed, chanting "Om, om, om." Very hypnotic. Very relaxing. Ben had almost zoned out himself waiting for the class to finish.

He was zoning a little now. He looked up, across the circle. Sue had her eyes closed. Her face was bathed in the orange glow from the amulet. She looked kind of peaceful. He looked to his right. So, surprisingly, did Reed. Reed, doing sorcery. For a second, it seemed strange to him, highly unlikely, but then he remembered something Stretch had told him once about higher-order theoretical physics, that the concepts scientists were playing with now bore an uncanny resemblance to the philosophies mystics and swamis from some Eastern religions had been playing with for hundreds, even thousands, of years. Science and sorcery, which, of course, made him think of Doom, made him look over Sue's shoulder, in the direction of the bubble and the hand that had broken through it earlier, but now all he could see was that glow. That orange color.

He looked to his left, at Olga. The amulet was glowing so brightly now she was barely visible through the haze.

Ben shut his eyes. All he could hear was the chanting, and beneath it, a low, insistent, thrumming, almost like machinery. Or the beating of a human heart.

"The power of the circle. The power of life itself."

He felt the glow from the amulet like a physical presence now, energy pulsing next to him, warmth spreading across his skin. It was peaceful. Relaxing. Like lying on the beach somewhere, basking in the hot afternoon sun, the rays beating down on him like a physical force.

It felt, Ben realized, like those first few minutes aboard the Mars ship, when the cosmic storm had come on them. That had been a pleasant feeling, too, at first—like warm raindrops landing all over his body. Like standing in a sun shower that had grown, bit by bit, into something stronger.

"What's happening to me?" he heard Sue say. "I feel so strange."

Ben opened his eyes. The glow was everywhere now, all around them. He couldn't see Sue—or the others, for that matter. He couldn't even see his own hands.

He could sure feel them, though.

They felt suddenly heavy. Too heavy to hold up.

His arms felt heavy, too.

His left hand slipped from Olga's grasp. His right followed a second later, tearing free of Reed's clutch, the cast slapping against the side of his thigh.

"Can't do it . . . anymore," he said, the words sounding strangely familiar in his head.

The others were still chanting.

"The power of the circle," they said. "The power of life itself."

Ben fell to his knees. This was exactly the same feeling he'd had on the Mars ship, only a hundred times worse. A thousand times worse.

He wondered where Max was. He wondered what was happening to him. It didn't feel like anything good.

He lay down on the floor and wanted to die.

"I feel so strange," a voice said. Sue. She sounded confused; she sounded scared.

Ben opened his eyes; even that was hard work. He saw Reed. He saw Olga.

But he couldn't see Sue anywhere; all he saw, in the spot where she'd been standing, was the orange. Reed was staring at that spot.

He was still holding Sue's arm, but the rest of her—

"Reed!" she yelled.

"Sue!" Reed yelled back. "What's happening to you?"

Ben wondered that, too, for a second. Then all he could think about was the pain again, the heaviness he felt in every square inch of his body.

His eyes closed.

He heard a sound behind him like the sudden roar of an engine flaring to life.

He smelled something burning and heard a scream. A man's voice. Not Reed, but not Doom, either. Then who . . .

"The power of the circle," Olga said, her voice all at once loud and clear. "The power of life itself."

The man stopped screaming.

"I'm on fire," he said. "I'm on fire again, but . . . I don't feel it. I don't feel a thing."

"Johnny?" Reed said.

No, Ben thought. *Johnny? Johnny Storm?*

He tried to turn his head—and found, to his surprise, that he could. The pain, the heaviness, seemed to be lessening, at least a little. Or maybe he was just getting used to it.

He opened his eyes, and where the voice had come from, he saw fire. A man on fire. *Tony,* he thought. Except it didn't quite look like Tony, there was something different about the color of the flame, the outline of the body underneath . . .

The drawing, Ben thought. The burning figure reminded him of the one in Max's drawing.

And with that thought, he felt a sudden chill run down his spine.

Oh, no, he thought. *Oh, God, no.*

The man on fire suddenly stopped burning.

It was Johnny. Alive, and whole.

Reed and Sue appeared next to him, holding hands and smiling.

"Johnny," Sue said, and then again, "Johnny!" and she ran to him and embraced him.

As they hugged, her body seemed, for an instant, to flicker in and out of existence. Visible one second, and not the next.

Johnny Storm, alive. For a second, Ben smiled.

"Kid," he managed, and then the three of them turned and looked at him, and the surprise and joy he saw in their eyes turned all at once to something else. Horror. And not a small amount of pity.

Even before Ben looked down at himself, at his arms and legs and body, gone suddenly massively heavy, he knew.

He knew, and he screamed.

16

HIS HANDS WERE ORANGE ROCK.

His arms, his legs, his chest were orange rock, too.

He did not want to see his face.

He got to his feet, the others still staring at him.

He felt thick, that was the only word for it. Massive. He couldn't even begin to guess how much he weighed, not that it mattered. He felt as if he could lift anything. As if he could take on the Hulk now, and Thor, and it would be an even match.

Alicia, he thought, and started to cry.

Johnny took a step back and flamed on again.

"Keep away," he said. "Whatever the hell you are, keep back, or I'll—"

"No," Sue said. "Don't. It's Ben."

It. Ben heard the word and screamed again.

"It's all right, Ben," Reed said. "It's okay. We're going to—"

"WHAT THE HELL PART OF THIS IS ALL RIGHT? WHAT ARE YOU TALKING ABOUT?" Ben screamed at the top of his lungs. "LOOK AT ME! LOOK WHAT HAPPENED, I'M A MONSTER!"

Olga, he thought, and turned to her.

She was standing in the exact same spot. She had, he realized, stopped chanting.

The amulet had stopped glowing. So, too, had the bubble around them.

"What did you do?" Ben asked, striding toward her. "What did you do to me?"

Even his voice sounded different. Thicker, harsher. The words slurred, as if he had to try harder to move his tongue and mouth to shape them. The building shook with every step he took. He had to weigh a ton, at least.

They were going to need to reinforce the house. They were going to need new doors.

The kids were never, ever going to look at him without screaming.

"It was the amulet," Olga said. "Not me."

He heard a sound like breaking glass, and turned.

The bubble had shattered.

Doom stood there, hands—one hand, rather, one claw—on hips, facing them.

"This is how it should be, I suppose," he said. "The four of you, and I. Order versus chaos."

He snapped his fingers, and the amulet around Olga's neck suddenly ripped free and flew into his hands. Doom secreted it inside his cloak.

"I don't see how it's a fair contest at all, truthfully."

Ben charged right at him.

Doom waved a hand, and a shield of light appeared before him. The same one, Ben realized, he'd bounced off before.

He didn't bounce this time.

He ran smack into it. The shield and the air around it shuddered and moved.

Doom moved as well, with some urgency, touching his hand to the gold belt around his waist.

Ben, pushing against the force shield, felt it suddenly stiffen and stabilize.

"What kind of thing are you?" Doom asked.

"The kind of thing that's going to twist you into a pretzel," Ben said, and raised his hands to strike the force shield, and all at once, Doom was in his head again.

He staggered back.

But every part of him was stronger now.

Ignoring the pain, he smashed the force shield again, with all his might, remembering as he did so the cast on his right hand, but of course the cast wasn't there anymore, and neither was the break. All there was was rock. Orange rock. Invulnerable rock.

The shield broke, and Doom staggered backward.

"Not much of a contest is right," Ben said, and reached for the man.

Doom raised his hands above his head, and suddenly, the roof above them split, and light poured down from the heavens.

Not just light, Ben realized a split second later. Energy.

Doom seemed to grow before his eyes.

"There is a crack in reality," he said, and hit Ben with his claw.

Ben flew backward across the room and smacked into the wall. The building shook.

"Beneath that crack," Doom said, advancing on the five of them, "is power. Primordial power. The stuff that shapes the universe. And it is mine."

"Victor, you know we have to fix the crack," Reed said. He put Sue and Olga behind him. "We have to put things back the way they were."

"I don't think so," Doom said. "I don't think we have to fix it at all."

Reed's eyes narrowed. "You want to destroy the machine."

"I want to destroy everything," Doom said. "Starting with you."

The air crackled with power. Ben launched himself forward, but too late.

Beams of energy shot from Doom's hands, right toward his friends.

They stopped, inches short of their target, and scattered, as if they'd hit some kind of shield. An invisible shield, like Doom's.

"What is this?" Doom asked.

Magic, Ben thought, and looked to Olga. But she huddled behind Reed, barely visible.

Sue, on the other hand . . .

Her brow was lined, her face furrowed in concentration.

"Of course," Doom said then. "The girl."

"Sue?" Reed asked, and looked to her. "What are you—how are you doing this?"

"I don't know," she said.

"It doesn't matter," Doom said, and he lunged forward suddenly, slashing at the shield.

Sue gasped.

"You will all be dead soon."

"You leave my sister alone," Johnny said, and suddenly his flame, which had died down a little, surged to life again, hotter than before, hotter, Ben realized, than Yates had ever been. So hot he had to take a step back.

"Take it easy, kid," he said. "Don't burn us up, too."

"Don't worry. I know what I'm doing." Johnny advanced on Doom, and the heat went with him. Fire burst from his hands, and at Doom, who fell back, reeling from the attack.

The kid is a natural, Ben thought. How long had it taken Yates to learn how to control his power like that?

Months, at least. And here Johnny was doing it minutes after . . .

But it wasn't minutes, he realized, remembering the drawing.

It was Johnny's whole life—his life as it was supposed to be, apparently.

And with that thought, he realized something else. His body, his size, the weight he had to lug around . . .

He barely noticed it at all now. What did that say about who—what—how—he was supposed to go through the rest of his days?

"That shield of yours," Reed said to Sue. "Can you modify its shape?"

Sue frowned. "I don't know. I have no idea how it works."

"I think you can," Reed said. "Because it makes sense, logically, if we look at what's happening to you—this ability to refract light, to bend it away, to control the waves and the particles that—"

"Stop, Reed. I don't understand what you're talking about," Sue said.

"But I do," Reed said. "You just have to trust me."

Then he told her what he wanted her to do.

When he was done, Sue looked at him, and for a second, Ben thought she was going to argue, the way Yates would. Or talk about alternative strategies, probabilities, the way Max always liked to.

Instead, she threw her arms around Reed and kissed him.

"I love you," she said. "I haven't stopped loving you since the day I walked out of your apartment, and I will never stop. Never. Ever. No matter what."

Reed opened his mouth to reply, and frowned a moment. "I agree," he said finally. "With every sentiment you just expressed. I feel the same way, only this is not necessarily the time or place to . . ."

"Enough with the hearts and flowers, already," Ben said. "What are we doing, Reed? What's the plan?"

"What are we doing?" Reed smiled at Sue, and then his face grew deadly serious.

"We're killing Doom," he said. "That's what we're doing."

Johnny, at that second, hurtled past them, his flamed suddenly doused.

"The machine, Richards," Doom said, coming toward them again. "Where is it?"

"Step right in front of us, Ben," Reed said. "Protect Sue. No matter what, protect Sue."

Ben did as he had asked, not a second thought, either, putting himself right between Doom and the others. Now, more than ever, he felt invulnerable. As if nothing—no one, not even Doom—could hurt him.

"On my word," Doom said. "I will give you your family. I will give you an island of reality, one that will stand for all eternity, ceaseless and unchanging, no matter the chaos that goes on without."

"Shut up," Ben said.

"Your family forever," Doom continued, "if you stand aside now."

Ben heard whispering behind him. A second later, he felt heat.

Johnny shot by, to the far end of the room.

Doom spun to watch him for a second, then turned back.

"The same offer to you, Richards. You and Susan. Together forever, if you tell me where the machine is."

"Now, Sue," Ben heard Reed say.

And Doom screamed.

He looked down at his chest, at the hole the Max androids had blasted into him. Ben looked, too. That hole, he saw, was getting wider. Sue's invisibility shield, he realized.

"Push it through him," Reed said, louder this time. "Expand it."

The hole grew, and a second later, Doom screamed again.

He was, literally, being ripped in half.

He made a gurgling noise in his throat and pointed his arm.

Blue fire shot from it and hit Ben square in the chest. It hurt like a sonuvagun.

It hurt so much he doubted Mister Invulnerable would have been able to stand the pain. But he wasn't Mister Invulnerable anymore. Now he was someone different. Some *thing.*

The word rang in his heart.

Thing. He thought, for some reason, of the hand from the Addams Family, and almost—almost—smiled.

"No!" Doom screamed, and swung his arm in a circle. The fire hit the walls, the elevator, everywhere, and wherever it hit, wherever something had been, there was now nothing.

Doom fell to his knees.

He raised his hands above his head, the way he had before, when the energy had replenished him, but suddenly, Johnny was there. The energy, wherever it was coming from, surged toward Doom, and then away from him, as it hit the heat shield that Johnny made.

Doom screamed again. "Richards!"

He swung his arm in a circle one more time, and then he stopped swinging it altogether.

He crouched there, chest heaving, gasping for breath. Like a wounded, dying animal.

"You're a peasant," Doom managed. "I am a king, a king. This . . ."

He stopped talking and bowed his head.

"Reed," Ben heard Sue say behind him. "Shouldn't we . . ."

He could hear it in her voice. She wanted to stop.

"We have to finish it, Sue," Reed said, not a trace of doubt or hesitation in his voice.

Ben risked a glance behind him.

Reed had a hand on Sue's shoulder. Her eyes were shut tight, her brow furrowed in concentration.

Reed smiled at Ben—a thin, tight smile with no joy in it.

"Do it," he said to Sue. "Do it now."

She nodded and, once more, didn't argue or try to talk Reed out of it.

Ben looked at her, then at Reed, and then turned and looked back at Johnny.

A team, Ben thought. *We're working like a team.*

It was a new feeling, and yet . . .

A familiar one, too.

Doom screamed again, and Ben could hear the pain in his voice.

He almost—almost—felt sorry for the man.

Doom started crawling toward them.

"Peasants," he groaned, his voice like sandpaper. "Gnats. I will crush you."

He reached Ben's feet and extended a hand. Two fingers, and a claw.

It landed next to Ben's foot and lay there.

Doom lay there, too, for a long minute, breathing heavily.

And then the breathing stopped.

"Hey!" Johnny shouted from across the room. "Is that it?"

Reed peered out from behind Ben and looked down at the cloaked figure, motionless on the floor.

"I think so," he said. "I think—"

Doom snarled and slashed upward with the claw.

It caught Reed right in the gut, and his shirt exploded with crimson.

He gasped and fell backward. Reed looked up at Ben, his eyes wide in shock and pain.

Sue screamed.

"Now," Doom hissed. "Now, it's finished."

He collapsed on the floor.

Ben screamed, then hit Doom with all his strength. His fist smashed into Doom, and through him. The floor shook.

Ben turned around. Sue was holding Reed's head in her lap.

Johnny had flamed off and was standing over them.

"In a minute," Sue said, "I'm going to have Johnny go upstairs to your medical lab, and we're going to get a—"

Reed shook his head. "Don't have a minute."

He looked up at Sue and managed a smile. She was crying, Ben saw.

"Glad," Reed said. "Glad I found you again. And we stopped him. Doom. You and I, together."

"Don't talk," Sue said. "Save your strength. Johnny, go to the medical lab and get me . . ."

"Sue, I don't know where the medical lab is," he said.

"I do," Ben said. "What does he need, Suzy? Tell me what he needs."

She opened her mouth, and Reed made a gasping, rattling sound in his throat.

"Reed?" Sue said, and touched his shoulder gently.

He didn't move.

"Reed?"

He didn't need anything, Ben saw. Not now, not ever again.

He stood up and punched the wall, harder than he'd intended.

The wall shook. Plaster dust fell down on them.

"Hey," Johnny said. "We got troubles enough already, don't you think?"

Ben turned and glared at him. "Listen, match head," he said, and stopped, because all at once he was struck by a sense of déjà vu more powerful than anything he'd experienced in . . . well, in several days at least.

"Match head?" Johnny said.

Ben frowned. He didn't know where the word had come from, either.

"Wait," Sue said suddenly, and went to Doom's cloak, and searched through it frantically until she found what she was looking for.

She held the amulet up.

"Come on," she said. "All of you. Join hands. The power of the circle. The power of life itself."

Ben looked at her and smiled.

"It's no use." Olga, whom Ben had completely forgotten about, who'd stood there silently, helplessly, this whole time, shook her head sadly.

"What do you mean, it won't work?" Sue demanded. "We just saw—Johnny, and . . ."

Olga just kept shaking her head.

"It's just," she began, and Ben knew what she was going to say even before she spoke. "It won't work twice."

"He's not dead," Sue said, her voice shaking. "I did not come here, I did not go through all this, just so that Reed . . ."

She bit her lip and stopped talking.

She turned away from the rest of them, and her shoulders began to shake.

Ben took a step toward her and stopped himself.

He didn't think being held by a guy made of orange rock would rate high on the list of comforting moments.

"Sue," Johnny said, and went to her.

Ben watched them a moment, then gazed down on Reed and Doom, both motionless on the floor.

Doom was right, he thought. *It was finished.*

And then he realized it wasn't. Not just yet, anyway.

"The crack in reality," he said out loud.

Both Sue and Johnny turned to him.

"Huh?" Johnny said.

"We have to find the machine," Ben said. "The Q-Ray. And then we have to . . ."

He frowned. Reed had died before telling him what, exactly, they had to do.

He ran—well, ran for two steps, strode quickly for the rest, as the two running steps he took shook the building in a way that he didn't think was good for the already weakened structure—from the rubble of the reception room into the rubble of the staging area.

Yates lay where he had fallen. Ben knelt down next to him and checked his wrist for a pulse. Nothing. But he wasn't sure he could feel a pulse with his fingers, anyway. His four fingers. Each hand had only four fingers.

"Ben." He looked up. Sue stood over him.

"Let me."

"Yeah," he said, and stood and stepped aside.

Sue couldn't find a pulse, either.

"So what do we do now, Ben?" she asked.

He thought a minute.

Yates was dead. Reed was dead. Max was . . . where?

He hadn't been in the building, Doom had said that, but then . . . he'd sent the hologram, sent the other androids to attack Doom, which meant that he was. Except they hadn't heard a word from him since, which meant he was either hurt or . . . gone again. But why would he abandon them in the middle of their fight against Doom? What could possibly be more important than . . .

"Oh," Ben said out loud.

"What?" Sue asked.

"The machine," Ben said. "The Q-Ray."

"You wanna talk in complete sentences?" Johnny asked.

"Max is using the machine," Ben said. That was the

only explanation that made sense, that was why Reed had looked so worried when he found out the Max with them was an android. *We agreed, and Max fooled me,* Reed had said, meaning Max wasn't going to do what Reed wanted. That Max had only been pretending to agree with him, that, in fact, Max had ideas, and wishes, and plans of his own, and thinking about it like that, Ben knew why.

The Mad Thinker. The strand that was.

"We have to stop him," Ben said.

"He's your buddy," Johnny said. "Your teammate, right? Why would he want to . . ."

"Kid, it's complicated," Ben said, and turned on his heel and headed for the command center.

Every screen in the room was dark. Main power was down.

"What are you doing?" Johnny asked.

"Before we can stop him, we gotta find him," Ben said. "We gotta find the machine."

"Reed's the only one who knows—who knew—where it was," Sue said.

"I'm betting Max knows, too. That he figured out where Reed hid it. I'm hoping—ah," Ben said, as he found the service panel and brought the backup power on-line. The system began to boot up.

Ben rolled a chair over in front of the screen and sat down. Or tried to, anyway. His butt wouldn't fit.

He rolled the chair out of the way and stood over the input panel.

"I'm hoping we can figure it out, too," Ben said. "That we can find some info in the system that'll give us a clue, or . . ."

The screen before him came to life. It flashed a prompt:

PASSWORD?

Ben carefully pecked in his access code.

INCORRECT INPUT.

He tried again, thinking maybe he had hit a wrong key, and got the same result back.

"He changed the password," Ben said. "Max changed the password."

Johnny leaned over his shoulder. "Take some guesses," he said.

Ben turned toward him and snorted. "Guesses? What do you mean?"

"I mean, most people, when they set up passwords, they use simple ones. Ones easy for them to remember."

"Max is not most people."

"Yeah, but still . . . last few digits of his phone number, his middle name, his dad's name, his wife's name . . ."

"We can try it," Ben said, shrugging. "No harm in trying."

He tried *Rose.* He tried *von Scharf.* He tried the last four digits of Max's phone number, then Max's whole phone number. Nothing.

"Try a few more," Johnny urged. "What else about

him? His favorite number, his favorite color . . . come on. He's your buddy, right?"

Ben glared. He wished Johnny would stop saying that.

"It's not gonna work," he said, and turned away. Max was just as likely to have a sixty-nine-digit prime number or something as his password.

"We're gonna have to use our heads here," Ben continued. "We're gonna have to puzzle it out."

"Where the machine is," Sue said. "Reed said something about taking Yates down to see it, before . . . ?"

Ben nodded. He remembered that, too. But he didn't believe it; Reed had been on to Yates then, so *down* was misdirection, which meant *up*. The labs. But the labs were the first place Ben would have thought to look. Doom must have looked there, too. Doom, now that Ben thought about it, must have looked everywhere in the building before confronting them. So the machine wasn't in the building.

But that made no sense. Reed was going to take Yates there himself, and he hadn't made it sound as if the trip required a lot of extra effort. In the building, then, but . . . not in the building.

Ben frowned. Just like Max. In the building, but . . . not.

And then he smiled.

"What?" Sue asked.

"I know where they are," Ben said, and headed for the core. "The machine and Max."

Sue and Johnny made to follow him.

"No," Ben said.

"Why not?" Johnny asked.

"Because it's dangerous."

"Max, you mean?" Sue shook her head. "He'd never hurt us."

Ben shook his head. If what he suspected about Max's reasons for using the machine were true . . .

"I don't know about that. Besides, it's not just Max I'm worried about."

"So we're just supposed to stay here and twiddle our thumbs?" Johnny said.

Ben opened the door to the stairway. Dust swirled in the air. Part of the ceiling had collapsed, he saw. Getting to his destination was going to be a little tricky. Maybe he could use Johnny's help, at that.

And then he remembered where he was going and shook his head.

"You're supposed to work on Plan C," he said.

"Plan C?"

Ben nodded. "What to do if I don't come back."

He entered the core and shut the door behind him.

It took him, best guess, ten minutes to reach the next level of the building. Another ten to get to his destination. The door to the chamber was blocked by rubble. Ben cleared it, steel groaning as he moved each piece. For a second, he worried that the entire building would collapse.

Then the last of the rubble was clear, and he stood before the entrance.

DANGER
ABSOLUTELY NO ACCESS
DANGER

The keypad next to it was flashing red.

The Negative Zone. Where better to hide the machine than in another universe entirely.

He tried the usual access code. Changed, of course. Max didn't miss a trick.

He stepped back and looked at the door.

It and the locking mechanism were composed of adamantium. Hardest substance on the planet. Reed—and Max, if he was remembering right—had designed it to withstand a direct nuclear explosion and a full-on assault by the Hulk.

Time to see just how strong I am as a monster, Ben thought, and began hitting it.

Five minutes on, his hands were beginning to hurt, and the door looked untouched.

Ten minutes on, he could swear he was feeling the break in his right hand, where the cast had been—and the door was still untouched.

Brute force, clearly, wasn't going to work.

He made his way, through another stack of rubble, to Lab 4 and the observation window.

There was still only blackness before him, but that didn't mean much. This was an entire universe he was looking at it. A dead universe, to be sure, but still big enough to hide a million Maxes, a million Q-Rays.

He put his fingers on the glass.

This, Ben bet, he could break.

Only problem with doing that was that what lay beyond was antimatter, and if any of that touched any of the stuff in this world . . .

Well, the resulting explosion, at least as Ben understood it, would make the crack in reality that had destroyed Elizabeth look like a popgun going off.

He went back to the access door in the hall and stood before it a moment.

Maybe he should go get Johnny, have him try to burn his way in.

Maybe he should start beating on the door again.

Maybe, Ben reflected, he should trust Max. Let him use the Q-Ray. Let him try to fix things, whatever he was going to try to do. Let him save their lives—Alicia, and the kids, and Rose . . .

Ben frowned.

He turned to the keypad and punched in her name.

The door opened.

Ben stood there a second, feeling inordinately proud of himself. He'd just realized Max wouldn't have had much time to change the code on the door here, and Ben'd chosen the most likely combination Max would have used, and it had worked.

The second he stepped inside the chamber, he realized he'd also guessed right about where Max and the machine were.

The gateways were lit. The portals active.

Ben grabbed a jetpack off the wall and, after some difficulty—he was definitely not a 44 long anymore—managed to strap it on.

He passed through the portals and emerged onto the launch platform.

Beyond was the vast blackness of the Negative Zone.

Twenty feet in front of him was the Q-Ray, and, standing next to it, Max.

"Hello, Ben. That is you, isn't it?"

"Yeah, it's me." He reached back to take the jetpack off and stopped himself. The machine was powered on, he saw. And removing the pack would take precious seconds. "Move away from the machine."

"I'm afraid I can't do that Ben."

Now, Ben thought to himself. *Do it now.*

But part of him hesitated.

"The Mad Thinker. I won't become that person again. That monster. You, of all people"—and here, his eyes traveled up and down Ben's form—"you should understand."

I do, Ben almost said, but he closed his mouth on

his words, because if he responded to Max, Max would respond to him, they'd have an argument, it would turn into a conversation, and Ben knew—he just knew—that he would end up listening, end up getting talked out of what had to be done.

Ben took another step forward. "We have to put things back the way they're supposed to be, Max. You know that."

Max shook his head.

"That's not exactly right, Ben. All we have to do is fix the crack. And I have been working, working all night, on a way to do that." He smiled. "Everything is going to be fine. Trust me."

Ben leaped toward him. But not fast enough.

He saw movement—Max's hand on the machine's control panel. He saw a light flash.

His hand reached for his friend's, and then the world faded to black.

17

BEN OPENED HIS EYES.

Alicia was leaning over him, a smile on her face.

"Who's the sleepyhead now?" She leaned closer and kissed him. Her lips were soft and warm.

His lips were soft, too, Ben realized.

He sat up, so suddenly Alicia had to take a quick step back.

"Hey!" she said. "Careful."

Ben didn't answer for a second, just looked around, and down, and back at her, and then himself.

He was in their bedroom, in a T-shirt and sweats. His hand was in a cast. His skin was pink. He was human again. Completely, one-hundred-percent human.

A dream, he thought. *All that orange monster stuff, it was just a dream.*

He smiled.

But his heart was pounding like a jackhammer.

Alicia went to the window and drew the curtains.

"You must be famished," she said. "Steak and eggs?"

He looked at the clock. It was ten-thirty.

"Or you want to skip breakfast and go right to lunch?" Alicia asked, following his gaze.

"I guess I was tired."

"And no wonder. After the day you had." She smiled. Ben forced himself to smile back.

"Right," he said. "After the day I had."

Though for the life of him . . . he couldn't remember all that much about it.

He got out of bed. "I'm going to take a shower. I'll be down in a minute."

He turned and headed toward the bathroom.

"Max is downstairs," Alicia called after him. "He wants to talk to you."

Ben froze in midstep. Max.

A chill went down his spine.

Images flashed in his brain.

Doctor Doom, with hooves. Jembay Diehl. Olga, turning out to be some kind of sorceress.

Sue and Johnny Storm, turning out to be—members of the Fantastic Four, for all intents and purposes.

Yates dead. Reed dead. Him a monster, and Max . . .

"You all right, honey?" Alicia asked.

"Down in a minute," Ben said again, and went into the shower.

He turned the water on as hot as he could stand it, and stood there for several long minutes, making sense out of his memories and the images he kept seeing in his head. Then he got dressed and headed downstairs.

Max was sitting at the kitchen table, drinking a cup of tea. He rose at Ben's approach.

"There he is—Mister Invulnerable. How are you feeling, Ben?"

Ben avoided his eyes. "Better." He walked to the counter and poured himself a cup of coffee from the carafe.

"Quite a day yesterday," his friend said, coming up behind him. "Doom turning out to be behind it all. Elizabeth, Smolensk . . . I would never have imagined."

"Right," Ben said. "Me, neither."

"I'm glad it turned out all right in the end," Max said. "We can head into the city later, if you want. Review things with Reed and Tony."

Ben took a sip of his coffee and said nothing for a moment.

When he turned around, Max was still looking right at him.

"What else do you remember about yesterday, Ben?"

Ben hesitated.

He could just pretend nothing was wrong, he realized. Go on about his business. Live his life. Or . . .

Orange rock. Sue and Johnny Storm. The Mad Thinker.

The way things were supposed to be.

"What else do I remember?" Ben said. "Everything."

The two men stared at each other a moment.

Max shook his head and sighed heavily.

"I was hoping you wouldn't," he said. "I was hoping I would be the only one."

"Well, you're not," Ben said. "I remember it all. I remember what we were trying to do, what Reed was saying. The crack in reality, I remember—"

"There is no crack, Ben." Max smiled. "Not anymore. I fixed it. I fixed everything."

Ben frowned.

"You fixed it?"

"Down to the one hundred and fifty-sixth decimal place." He tapped the side of his head. "The equations work now, Ben. Everything works. You and I, we can stay here. Stay like this. We can—"

"Ben!" Alicia called from the living room. "Ben, come quick!"

He was through the door in a flash. "What's wrong? What . . ."

He stopped in his tracks.

Something in the room was different. It took him a second to figure out what.

"Hey," he said, looking around. "Where are the kids' things?"

Alicia stared at him as if he'd grown two heads.

"What?"

"The kids' things," Ben said again. "Tatianna's painting, Benjy's word puzzle . . ."

Alicia just kept looking at him strangely. "Kids? What on earth are you talking about, Ben?"

He looked at her, and then he looked at Max.

His friend took a minute before responding.

"I'm sorry, Ben, but in this strand . . . it appears that . . ."

Alicia put a hand on his arm.

"Are you sure you're all right, Ben? You want to lie down and rest a minute?"

"Sure," he said. "I'm fine. Peachy keen. What did you want to show me?"

"On the TV, I was just watching"—she pointed toward the flat-screen TV on the wall, which was showing a commercial now, and then she flicked the remote in her hand, and the channels started flashing by—"there," she said, anxiety evident in her voice. "There. You see?"

Ben looked at the screen.

There was an image of a dark cloud on a horizon—a cloud filled with flashes of what looked like all different colors of lightning. A little one-word line identifying the transmission ran along the bottom of the picture. It said: *Elizabeth, New Jersey.*

"Some kind of freak electrical storm, they said," Alicia continued. "A terrible one. Hundreds of people dead—maybe even thousands."

Ben closed his eyes.

"You two should go," Alicia said. "Find out what it is. Shouldn't you?"

"Yes," Ben said. "We should find out what it is, and fix it."

He turned and stared at Max.

"There was one variable," his friend began, "a forty-three-point-six-two-five-percent chance that there would be this kind of instability, but I know that variable's physical location. I can map it out so that . . ."

"No, Max," Ben said.

"Ben. Listen to reason. Forty-three point six percent—roughly—those are odds worth taking. Chances worth taking, because the alternative . . ."

"NO!" he said, and grabbed Max by the collar and shook him. "NO! NO! NO!"

He kept shaking. He kept yelling.

Alicia started yelling, too.

At some point, Ben looked down and saw that Max's eyes had rolled back in his head. He wasn't breathing.

He was, however, sparking.

It wasn't Max at all, he saw. It was an android.

Ben dropped it to the ground and headed for the door.

"Ben!" Alicia yelled after him. "Ben, what's wrong? What's wrong with you?"

He ignored her, because she wasn't real. She wasn't real, any more than the kids had been real, any more than Mister Invulnerable or Max von Scharf were real. Reality was the drawing. Reality was the Mad Thinker, and the thing that Ben had been. The thing he was on the way to becoming, once again, and forever.

He took the boat across the river; halfway across the Hudson, his commlink started beeping. Ben tossed it into the water.

At the Baxter Building, an O'Hoolihan stopped him at the front door. "I'm sorry, Mr. Grimm, but Mr. Richards and Mr. von Scharf gave me strict orders—"

He punched right through the android and kept walking, past the empty storefront where Theo's used to be, and right up to the elevator.

It wouldn't open for him. No surprise.

He went to the regular elevator bank and took the first car to the topmost floor.

He walked out of the car and turned right. A secretary tried to stop him; he ignored her. He burst through the first door to his right, which turned out to be a conference room, filled with men and women in business suits.

A little man stepped in his path.

"Hey. Ben Grimm. Mister Invulnerable, right? Geez, what are the odds of you coming into my office and—"

Ben pushed past the man, walked to the window at the end of the room, and smashed through the glass.

He stepped outside, onto the ledge of the building, and began to climb.

Outside the Level A windows, two of the modified Robertas attacked. He made short work of them.

Then a streak of fire burst past. Yates.

"Reed says you're not allowed in, Ben," Yates called down. "He and Max were talking, they said you—"

Ben shut him up—and extinguished his flame—with a huge handclap that created a sonic boom, a wind that not only sent Yates tumbling toward the ground but also smashed open the window behind him.

Alarms were sounding as he entered the staging area. Androids charged.

He made short work of them, too.

Reed came out of the command center, holding a hypo. Part of Reed, anyway—one arm, head and shoulders, the other arm stretching behind—

Ben turned and grabbed that other arm by the wrist, as it snuck up behind him.

He twisted.

Reed grunted in pain. "Ben. Don't make this any harder than it has to be. This delusion . . ."

"Not a delusion," Ben said. "The Q-Ray."

Reed frowned. “That’s experimental. How did you . . .”

Ben told him. Everything.

Reed looked stunned when he finished. Shocked.

“Then Sue and I . . .” he said, and smiled.

He looked back at Ben, and the smile disappeared from his face.

“Whatever happens to you, cosmic ray mutation is a reversible genetic process. In theory, if I can . . .”

“You can’t,” Ben said, and pushed past him, heading for the core. He climbed the stairs and entered the Negative Zone chamber.

Max was frantically pushing buttons on the machine.

“No, no, no,” he said. “Ben, listen to me. I know what I did wrong. There is a set of variables I failed to account for, if you give me a few more minutes.”

Ben pulled his hands off the controls. “I can’t, Max. I’m sorry.”

“So am I, Ben.”

He pulled something out of his pocket then. It looked like a little blue pen.

He pointed it at Ben, and blue fire shot through the air.

Ben lost control of his limbs and fell to the ground.

He lost control of everything for a minute; the world went herky-jerky on him.

Time—a few seconds, a few minutes, Ben didn’t know for sure—passed.

He opened his eyes.

Max was at the controls again, mumbling to himself. The machine, Ben saw, was glowing now.

"A subzero," Max said. "*B* is the secondary variable, *C* the third—"

Ben struggled to his feet. Max turned and saw him.

"Almost there," he said, and smiled again. "You'll see. This time, I'm right. This time . . ."

Ben had the strangest sense of déjà vu. This had happened before, maybe, he thought. Maybe a lot of different times, this had happened.

"Sue," Max said. "We'll make her part of the team as well—that's actually a stabilizing factor, as it turns out, because it's Reed who discovers . . ."

Ben didn't want to hear any more.

He lunged forward. His hand hit the machine.

The glow got brighter.

He pushed Max's hand off the controls.

"No!" Max shouted. "If I don't meet you, if I don't meet Reed . . . I'll be a monster, Ben. A monster."

"You and me both, buddy," Ben said, and grabbed a dial at random.

Max's hand touched his, and . . .

Interlude two

Ben drifted in the blackness of the exclusionary Hilbert space, somehow knowing exactly where he was and what he had to do. But before he did it . . .

He wanted, for one last time, to remember.

And so he floated, and spun the world around him, time and time again, until he found what he was looking for.

A string of light—a strand that, when he pulled it closer, or caused it somehow to move toward him, looked like nothing so much as a strip of film, a row of pictures, of scenes, passing before his eyes.

And after a time, he found the one he was looking for.

Himself and Alicia, sitting together and smiling. Sitting in a row alongside dozens, no, hundreds, of other people. They were in a stadium somewhere, which made him frown. Alicia didn't like sports, except maybe ice-skating.

He was older. So was she. They were wearing sweatshirts, ESU sweatshirts, and holding little banners in their hands, and cheering. On their feet now, and cheering, as was everyone else around them. It was a stadium, Ben saw. A football stadium.

Whatever game had been going on was ending. He and Alicia stayed in the stands—people came by and congratulated them on their way out. He was beaming, Ben saw. The Ben in the scene he was watching was beaming, and shaking hands, and as he turned, Ben saw the sweatshirt that he wore had a number on the back, 56, which had been his number in college.

And then a football player bounded up the seats toward Alicia, and hugged her, and Ben, the Ben drifting in the Hilbert space, suddenly realized what he was seeing.

It was Benjy. Benjy, who hated football, who wouldn't even play catch with him in the backyard, was wearing his old number and playing for his old school.

He saw son turn to father then, and the two embraced.

"You did all right, kid," he heard himself say.

"All right?" Benjy punched him on the shoulder. "Fifteen tackles, and just all right?"

They embraced again, and the scene suddenly changed.

Ben saw his brother, Dan, seated at a courtroom table, looking older, too, gray hair, lines on his face, thicker through the body. He was sitting next to a young woman, who was reading a note he was writing on a yellow legal pad. Ben shifted the scene, so that he could read the note, too.

"Clobberin' time," it said.

The young woman smiled, pushed her chair back, and stood.

"Ladies and gentlemen of the jury," she began. "The prosecution's case is illusory. It is filled with holes," she said, her finger jabbing at the air, "and I will now point out each and every one of them."

Ben took a closer look at her.

Tatianna?

All at once, he sensed a presence nearby, and spun the world again.

Max?

He heard his friend's voice in his mind.

Ben, don't do this. I can fix it.

He didn't respond.

He pictured Alicia, in his mind, lying next to him in bed, sitting beside him at the breakfast table, waiting for him in the foyer when he walked in the door at night. The expression on her face, that first moment in the hospital, when she'd looked at him and seen him, actually seen him, for the very first time.

Is it Reed? Are you worried about Reed? You needn't be. I know how to work the strands now—we can make it so that he and Sue—

He pictured Benjy and Tatianna, as babies, as children, and grown.

You won't even remember them, you know. There'll be nothing left of the memory, no trace of—

"I don't want to remember," Ben responded. "Now all I want to do is forget."

He spun the world again, slowly at first, and then faster.

Strings flew around him, gossamer-thin strands of light, like spiderwebs caught in the wind. He saw faces, familiar and unfamiliar, fly past. He heard voices in his mind.

Sue.

". . . got to take that chance, Ben, unless we want the Commies to beat us."

Johnny.

". . . only one thing I like more than racing cars."

Reed.

". . . together we have more power than any humans have ever possessed."

He found the strand he was looking for, and moved it closer.

He saw a blind girl, and a monster made of orange rock, and with his mind he reached out, and the black void began to fill with life.

18

THE WORLD TOOK SHAPE AROUND HIM.

He was in the visitor area, on C level. Where the lab was, and for a second, that seemed wrong to him. The visitor area was on B, right next to the command center, and no civilians were allowed in the command center. That was rule number one.

Whose rule, he—all at once—couldn't remember.

But the rules weren't important right at this instant. What was important was the man—and the machine—before him. The man who had his hand on the operating controls of the Q-Ray. The Mad Thinker, who was about to use Reed's machine in ways Reed had never intended, which Ben couldn't allow.

Except . . .

The Mad Thinker was just standing there, all of a sudden, looking at Ben with the oddest expression on his face.

Sadness.

"Rose," he said.

And Ben, whose own hand—four fingers, orange rock—was clasped tight around the Thinker's upper arm, froze where he stood.

Rose, he thought. There was something . . .

He pictured a little girl and a boy, holding hands. Walking in snow.

A woman in his kitchen. Speaking his name: *Benjamin.* No one ever called him Benjamin, except his grandmother, and she was dead and buried ten years ago.

And all at once, the sadness he saw in the Mad Thinker's eyes, the first honest, human expression he'd ever seen from the man . . .

Ben felt it, too.

The two men stood there a moment, staring at each other.

"Ben!" That was Reed's voice. "What are you waiting for, stop him before he—"

Ben drew his arm back and hit the machine.

He hit it once, twice, a dozen times, until the metal was crumpled, and the machine had stopped glowing, until it was so broken and battered that, clearly, it would be a long time, if ever, before it was functional again. He hit it without even knowing why he was doing it.

When he was done—when it was done—Ben stood over it, breathing heavily, feeling nothing other than that same sense of sadness he got from looking at the Thinker.

Reed came up alongside him. His friend, Ben saw, was tight-lipped.

His friend was furious.

"I hope," Reed began, "you have a good explanation as to—"

"An exclusionary Hilbert space," Ben said, and then pointed at the Thinker. "Like he said."

Reed, obviously still angry, opened his mouth to retort . . .

And then closed it again.

"Hmmm," he said out loud. "There is a possibility . . ."

A few feet away, Sitwell sat up and rubbed his neck.

"Ow," he said.

Ben looked around the room. The army and air force guys were helping each other to their feet. Starting to clean up.

Reed nodded to the Thinker. "Let's get him back to Rikers. You can handle it?"

"I can handle it," Ben said, and took the Thinker's arm.

The man looked at Ben again and managed a small smile. Not his usual mad-scientist, I'm-going-to-kill-you-all smile. A sad smile. An if-only smile . . .

"I had a dream," he said quietly, so no one else could hear. "You were in it."

That was not the kind of thing he was used to hearing from supervillains.

Ben opened his mouth to make a smart remark . . .

And for some reason, held his tongue.

He suddenly wondered what the Thinker would look like cleaned up. Hair combed back, different clothes . . . for a second, he could picture the man in his mind. He'd be a completely different person.

"You two done making nice yet?" Ben looked up and saw one of the S.H.I.E.L.D. guys standing over him. "'Cause there's a cell with this guy's name on it waiting."

Ben and the Thinker looked at each other.

"Yeah," he said. "We're done."

The S.H.I.E.L.D. guy escorted the Thinker out.

"What was that all about?" Johnny asked. "You two getting all buddy-buddy there?"

Ben shrugged.

"I don't know," he said. "It's this place, I guess. It has an effect on people."

The phone rang. Across the room, Sue answered it.

"It's for you, Ben," she said. "Alicia. She wants to know if you're interested in a concert tonight."

He crossed the floor to take it.

Reed knelt down next to the remains of the Q-Ray,

shaking his head and frowning, paying absolutely no attention to the world around him.

Ben turned his back on the others, and spoke into the phone.

"Hey," he said.

"Hey yourself. Are you busy?"

"Not anymore. What's up?"

"I have tickets to a concert, if you're interested."

Ben frowned.

"Jazz," Alicia said.

He smiled.

"If you're up for it."

"I'm on my way."

"You know where to find me," Alicia said, and hung up.

Acknowledgments

Wherever you all are:

Thanks to Donald Mills, Neil Cauley, Peter Engels, and Norman Brodesser. Thanks, too, to Bonzo de Kordova, for riding the rails with me, and the Passaic Book Store, for mailing the packages. To my dad, for taking me to Creation Con 72 to buy FF #2 and #3. To Margaret, for asking me if I was interested in writing a book on the FF. To Marvel, for being interested in the outline I made. To Brian Michael Bendis, for the *Ultimate Fantastic Four,* which I was very pleased to have discovered in the course of writing this book.

And finally, and most important, thanks, appreciation, and acknowledgment to Stan Lee and Jack Kirby.

—Dave Stern
—R.F.O., K.O.F.